Master New York ... to the town of Horsesh... ...der. Immediately he ran afoul of Barry Christian, the outlaw genius who terrorized Horseshoe Flat just as he did the entire West. Taxi is marked for destruction—until he gains the friendship of Arizona Jim Silver.

The legendary Silvertip has been on Christian's trail for years. Always the renegade is just within Silvertip's grasp, only to escape at the last moment. But now Christian is threatened by the strange partnership of Silvertip and Taxi—the brilliant lawman and the cunning criminal he has reformed.

Warner Books

By Max Brand

The Gentle Gunman
Dan Barry's Daughter
The Stranger
Mystery Ranch
Frontier Feud
The Garden of Eden
Cheyenne Gold
Golden Lightning
Lucky Larribee
Border Guns
Mighty Lobo
Torture Trail
Tamer of the Wild
The Long Chase
Devil Horse
The White Wolf
Drifter's Vengeance
Trailin'
Gunman's Gold
Timbal Gulch Trail
Seventh Man
Speedy
Galloping Broncos
Fire Brain
The Big Trail
The White Cheyenne
Trail Partners
Outlaw Breed
The Smiling Desperado
The Invisible Outlaw
Silvertip's Strike
Silvertip's Chase
Silvertip
Showdown
Smugglers' Trail
The Rescue of Broken Arrow
Border Bandit
The Sheriff Rides
Gunman's Legacy
Valley Vultures
Marbleface
The Return of the Rancher
Mountain Riders
Slow Joe
Happy Jack
Brothers on the Trail
The Happy Valley
The King Bird Rides
The Long Chance
The Man From Mustang
Mistral
The Seven of Diamonds
Dead or Alive
Smiling Charlie
Pleasant Jim
The Rancher's Revenge
The Dude
Riders of the Plains
The Jackson Trail
The Iron Trail
Pillar Mountain
The Blue Jay
Silvertip's Search
Silvertip's Trap
Silvertip's Roundup
Outlaw's Code
Montana Rides!
Montana Rides Again
Outlaw Valley
The Song of the Whip
Tenderfoot

MAX BRAND

Silvertip's Roundup

A Warner Communications Company

WARNER BOOKS EDITION

ISBN 0-446-88686-6

This Warner Books Edition is published by arrangement with Dodd, Mead & Company

Cover art by Carl Hantman

Warner Books, Inc., 75 Rockefeller Plaza, New York, N.Y. 10019

 A Warner Communications Company

Printed in the United States of America

Not associated with Warner Press, Inc. of Anderson, Indiana

First Printing: September, 1970

10 9 8 7 6 5

CHAPTER I

Horseshoe Flat

To "Taxi," the town of Horseshoe Flat looked cold. As the train departed, he remained on the station platform, staring until there was only a thin puff of smoke far away and a faint humming of the rails. Horseshoe Flat seemed empty. It stood all alone. The mountains around it were spectators, not a part of the scene. The day was hot enough, but the mountains were chiefly blue and white, and the sky came down too close to the ground.

There was nothing to cast shadows. The houses were too small, too far apart. There were no narrow alleys to offer mouths of twilight to one who does not desire too much observation. There were no lofty buildings cut into thin slices of regularly spaced windows, every building a wilderness where a cunning man could lose himself. There were no closely joining fields of roofs all at about one level, broken with skylights, ventilators, a forest of chimneys, where one could skulk as through a forest.

No, Horseshoe Flat seemed to be held up to the eye like a small coin in the palm of a hand. There was too much sky; there was too much light. Taxi didn't like it.

Then he remembered that he had a good pair of automatics under his coat and that his stay need not be long. Joe Feeley had been dead barely five days. Taxi had caught the first train out of New York to come West—the first train after he saw the news in the papers. And as soon as the killer of Joe Feeley was dead, Taxi could go home again.

He picked up his suitcase and walked to the corner of the platform. There sat the station agent on a hand truck, chewing a toothpick and looking at Taxi with curious eyes. Station agents are always curious. They seemed to know that sooner or later a policeman might come along and say: "Did you see a man about five feet ten, with black hair and kind of pale eyes? About twenty-three or four. You'd remember him by his eyes." That was the curse of Taxi's life—his eyes. He could fix himself in other ways, but he could not fix his eyes. That was why he had been in prison for ten years out of the twenty-two he had lived—prison or reform school.

Now he said to the station agent: "How d'you get uptown?"

The station agent pointed down. "Got sore feet?" he asked.

Taxi was about to look him in the face, but instinct saved him. He had learned years ago that it is better not to look people in the face; then they don't have a chance to see that you have pale eyes.

Back there in the "Big Noise" it meant something when Taxi looked a man suddenly and coldly in the face. When Taxi "gave a man the eye," the other fellow was apt to move right on out of town, if he had his wits about him. But even out here it was best to be careful, so Taxi swallowed the discourtesy and walked up the street.

As the weight of the suitcase pulled down on his arm, he was glad that he was in training, though it was not for carrying suitcases that he slaved in a gym. It was because, on three or four occasions in every free year, he could be sure that the speed of a sidestep, the ability to give wings to his heels, or perhaps his skill in climbing up the outside of a building, would mean money or life to him. That was why he had to keep himself in good shape.

It was a wretched business heaving medicine bags, climbing ropes, wrestling with ponderous fellows who had fifty pounds plus on him, or going through grueling rounds with the gloves. He never could please "Paddy" Dennis until he "went crazy." Whenever he "went crazy," Paddy used to jump out of the ring and lean on the ropes, laughing at him.

"You've got the stuff, kid," Paddy would say on occasions like that. "You've got the stuff in your pocket, but you hate to spend it. That right hook's a nacheral. *You're* a nacheral. When you go nutty, you're too nacheral for me!"

That was the way Paddy used to talk. But Taxi never wanted to "go crazy." He felt it was bad for him. It was bad for his brain, his nerve centers, his control. It may be all right to "go crazy" when you're using your fists and you have a target as big as a man at arm's length, but it's bad to "go crazy" when you're using a revolver and the other fellow is across the street. That is delicate work, the sort of delicate work that Taxi had to be in shape for every day he spent outside of prison. It must be all cool brains and speed and steady nerves, if you want to get your man. Taxi had got his man before, and he was in Horseshoe Flat to get another. But he forgave the deadly bore of the gymnasium as he walked up the street on this day, carrying the solid weight of the suitcase.

The newspaper office was so small that he almost went by it. Imagine a newspaper office like that!

He turned in and asked for a file. The red-headed girl who talked to him looked him right in the face. She put her hands on her hips and looked at him.

What sort of a woman was she to stare like that?

"Are you a traveling salesman? Is that why you wanta see the file?" she asked.

"I've traveled some," said Taxi. He had to look back at her. The way she was staring, he had to glance back at her, but he kept his eyes rather down so that the black of the long lashes would cover the paleness of his eyes.

She showed him where the file was, in a little cubbyhole of a room with the floor covered by cigarette butts.

"This is the devil of a town," said Taxi to himself, and sat down to look over the file.

He expected the paper which contained the account of the killing five brief days before would be thumbed to wrinkles. He was surprised to find it as crisp as any of the other copies. He scanned the first page and found nothing about Joe Feeley's death.

He looked up at the date, and found that it was right. Maybe they didn't write up the news the day after a thing happened. He looked at the next paper, but there was nothing about Joe on the front page. He turned back to the first copy. Nothing on the front page. Nothing on the second page. Nothing on the third page. Nothing on the fourth page—yes, down there beside the advertising on this inside page there appeared this account of Joe Feeley's death.

Afterward, he could remember it line for line.

NEW YORKER DIES

EASTERNER KILLED IN THE ROUND-UP BAR

> Last night at 11:15 in Porky Smith's Round-up Bar a stranger named Joseph Feeley ran into Charlie Larue. They didn't argue long. Charlie Larue fanned three shots through the stranger, and when Feeley was picked up, there was a gun in his hand that hadn't been fired.
>
> The bystanders said that there was some talk of a lady during the brief dispute. She was said to be Miss Sally Creighton, the popular young lady who runs the Creighton Boarding House. It appears that she went to a dance a few days ago with Mr. Feeley, and Mr. Larue seemed heated up about the idea.
>
> The deputy sheriff, Mr. Tom Walters, arrived shortly after the shooting. He decided that Joe Feeley had died in self-defense.

That was about all there was to the article.

Taxi decided that he would have to go out and look this town over from a new viewpoint. They seemed to be tough, in this part of the world. A man could die of self-defense, out here.

He remembered how the girl in the outer newspaper office had put her hands on her hips and stared at him. He felt that he could understand this better now.

He closed his eyes and found himself repeating the article. There were a few lines at the bottom which he had omitted. He opened the paper and regarded them again:

> Joseph Feeley will be buried some time today in the graveyard at the end of Lincoln Boulevard.

Taxi went out to the sidewalk with his hat pulled down over his eyes. The suitcase seemed to weigh nothing. And all he could see was the funny, long, laughing face of Joe Feeley. He had liked Joe Feeley. Joe Feeley was the sort of a fellow you could count on in a pinch, and he wasn't always shooting off his face about what he had done after the job was finished. Joe Feeley could drink his liquor and keep his mouth shut. He was that sort of a fellow. Plenty of fun, but no noise. No noise at the wrong moments.

Now, if Taxi could find Mr. Charlie Larue, the business might be quickly completed in this town where men died of self-defense!

There was something else to be attended to, first.

He asked for Lincoln Boulevard and was directed to it. The name was much grander than the fact. It was a long, straight, wide, dusty street. Aspiring citizens who wanted to make Horseshoe Flat bigger and better had planted trees along the sides and protected them with tall wooden cages. It looked as though some narrow-headed or long-tongued animals had been browsing off the foliage of these young trees. Those which were not chewed down had died from the lack of water.

Taxi walked to the foot of the street. Just at the point where Horseshoe Flat dissolved into open country, he found a barbed-wire fence around a plot of ground, and painted on the top board of a wooden gate were the words "Boot Hill Cemetery."

He paused and regarded it with care. He had heard of such a custom in the West, where an unknown victim of a gun fight might be put away at the public expense.

The more he thought about Horseshoe Flat, the less he liked it. The more he thought about Horseshoe Flat, the less he liked the people who lived in it.

He opened the gate and went inside. Grass grew knee-high in spots. It grew over a great many of the graves. He parted the grass with his feet and found tombstones. They were just chunks of stone with one side flattened by nature or chiseling, and into the stones a few words were generally chipped.

Here lies Dick Channery just the way Tony Fellows dropped him.

Or again he found:

Big Tim lies here. Slow Joe Murphy shrank him down to this size.

There was a fresh grave near the opposite fence. The soil had not been smoothed down. It simply lay in big, clayey shovelfuls, heaped above the surface and below the stone, blue-gray from the stone cutter's chisel, on which were marked the words:

Here's Joseph Feeley who caught Larue and died of it.

The date was underneath. There had been no date on most of the other graves.

"They're funny," said Taxi to himself. "They're damned funny."

He turned and looked with his pale, shining eyes at the town, and hated it. Some small boys were standing at the fence now. They pointed at him and laughed.

He hated the boys even. There was nothing to be said for this great, naked section of his native country. There was nothing to be said for the people who lived in it, either. Not even for the boys!

He turned back to the grave.

Somehow, he felt that something ought to be done, but he hardly knew what. He had had little experience.

Some of his friends had gone up Salt Creek, and the State took care of fellows like that. Some of them had simply disappeared. That was usually the way. One day you saw a fellow, and the next day he was gone. Nobody knew anything about it. After a while you knew he had been taken for a ride. That was all. Or else a fellow went out of town, to Chicago or Pittsburgh, or some place like that, and he never came back. But funerals were few and far between, and this was not even a funeral. It was just a stone with a joke on it, and a pile of clods over what had been a hole in the ground.

In the tangle of the grass there were some big blue flowers growing. He could not tell what they were. He knew nothing about flowers except what you find in the window of a florist's shop. Some of the fellows would pay a lot of money and send flowers like that to a girl. Taxi never did it. He had no girl.

But he picked some of these flowers. They had no fragrance, but only a green, rank smell. He picked quite a lot of them, and they made a big purple-blue bunch in his hand. When he put them on the raw, red clods, they looked rather silly, he thought. They looked as though the strength of the sun would wilt them in a few minutes. In fact, they seemed to be fading already.

He turned his back, because he did not want to see the flowers die on Joe's grave. He looked around him. It was a funny thing that Joe should lie here with the big mountains looking down at him with their blue-and-white faces.

CHAPTER II

Sally Creighton

WHEN Taxi left the Boot Hill Cemetery, one of the boys who had been watching him yelled out: "You a friend of that gent's?"

"Where's the Creighton Boarding House?" asked Taxi.

The lad took him there, babbling questions all the way. Taxi smiled, and said nothing. When he came to the boarding house, there was a sign in front of it, offering room and board for a ridiculously small price. It was strange that Joe Feeley should have picked up with a woman who ran a place like that. Joe was generally high class in his choice of females. But it's foolish to judge a man by his choice of a gun or a woman. Taxi had decided that long ago. It's just a matter of prejudice.

The boy knocked loudly at the door. Before the echoes

had stopped walking up and down inside, the door was pulled open by a girl whose face was rosy with heat. Her forehead was damp. Bits of her hair stuck to the skin and looked dark, though she was quite blond.

"Here's a gent that's a friend of the dead man!" cried the boy. "He wants to see you!"

The boy stood by and watched. He had his mouth and his eyes wide open.

"Run along, Willie," said the girl. She waved at the boy, but he stood fast.

"Come in," said the girl to Taxi.

He stepped inside. It was worse, to be near the girl. It made Taxi a little sick. He felt cold about the mouth, and he hated to look at her. If she had been a beauty, it would have been different, but she was nothing much. She had a good deal of color and light in her eyes, that was all; there was color in her hair, too. She had on a blue apron. The blue was faded at the knees. Her hair was all tousled. She looked like a poor drudge, except for the light and color in her eyes. There was something young and strong in her. The youth and the strength came up into her eyes and into her voice.

She led the way into a small front room. She raised a roller curtain. It went up with a rattle and let in a great, dusty shaft of sunshine out of the west. The sunshine fell on a carpet that had a pattern of red roses on it. The sunshine fell on the battered legs of an upright piano. There was a round, mahogany table in the middle of the room with some books held up between a pair of book ends. On the wall were some enlarged photographs. The faces seemed to watch Taxi.

"Sit down, please," said the girl.

He sat down on a plush chair, with his hat in his hand, his suitcase beside him. She sat down opposite him. He looked at the faded blue of the apron, across her knees. The apron was darkly splashed with water marks, and there was a white streak as of flour on it.

"Are you a relative of Joe Feeley?" she was asking him.

He kept looking at her knees, but through his lashes he could see her face, also. He knew how to do that without exposing the pallor of his telltale eyes.

"He's nothing to me," lied Taxi.

As he said it, he listened to himself and almost smiled. But if Joe Feeley had been near to listen in, Joe would have understood. That was the great thing about Joe. He understood. You could be silent for a week, but Joe always understood.

"I got word from a friend of Feeley's who knew I was coming out this way," said Taxi. "He asked me to look things over and find out what had happened. I read your name in the paper. That was all. So I came here to ask about it."

"I don't know anything about it," said the girl.

Taxi nodded. He kept his face as still as a stone. That was the way to talk to a stranger. You kept your face as still as a stone, and then nobody could get anything on you. You kept your face still, and remembered the shortest way your hands could get to your guns. Woman or man, it was always best to have no expression on the face.

The expression of the girl was growing cold, also. She was narrowing her eyes and staring at him the way people did in this part of the world. Everyone stared at you, as though they were all plain clothes men and suspected that something might be wrong.

But that was all right. That only made him feel a little more at home. That was the one home touch that he found in this town of Horseshoe Flat.

"It said in the paper," said Taxi, "that Feeley and a fellow called Larue had an argument about you and—"

He waited, letting his voice trail away, for the girl was sitting up straighter in her chair.

"Joe Feeley was a week in this house," she said. "That night he was lonely. He said he was very lonely. He asked me to go to the dance. I wasn't going to the dance, because I had to be up pretty early the next morning to cook a big breakfast for some people who were making a start. But I said I'd go, anyway. We went to the dance, all right. Charlie Larue was there. He had some sort of an argument with Feeley; I don't know about what."

Taxi nodded.

"Larue a friend of yours?" he asked.

"Yes. Rather a friend. I told Joe Feeley not to have

any trouble with Charlie Larue. I danced with Charlie, later on, and told him to remember that Joe Feeley was a stranger. Charlie said he would. But he didn't."

That was all. She sat back in her chair quietly, and waited. Taxi kept on looking at her knees and seeing her face.

"Feeley was new to this part of the world, the way I understand it," said Taxi. "I suppose he did a lot of things that he shouldn't have done. He made a lot of people mad. Was that it?"

"I liked him," said the girl. "I'll never put an eye on Charlie Larue again. I liked Joe Feeley. He was good-natured. He had a good laugh. But Charlie Larue started drinking, and that made the trouble. I think—"

She stopped. Taxi had heard the little click of her teeth and waited for her to go on.

"I'll take a room here, as long as I stay over," he said. "Have you got any rooms?"

She looked at him silently, nodding. She rose, and he rose with her, picking up his hat. At the door into the hall she paused and turned sharply. She was shaking her head.

"You'd better not," she said.

"Why not? What's the matter?" asked Taxi.

"You want to do something about Joe Feeley's death. Don't you try. You'd better pull out of the town and not try."

"I'm not going to do anything," said Taxi. "What could I do?"

"I don't know," she said. "You look quiet enough—in a way. But I want to warn you. Don't try to do anything to Charlie Larue."

She meant what she said. She had her chin up, like a person who means what he says.

"I only want to find out a few things," said he. "I simply want to find out what the trouble was about. That's all."

"I don't believe it," said the girl.

"And I'd like to have a room here, if you don't mind," he went on.

"Well—" She hesitated.

At last she led the way down the hall and opened a

door upon a big, empty room. He saw a patch of worn linoleum in front of a washstand, a brass bedstead, a colored calendar on the wall. The wall paper was peeling.

"This is the room that your friend Feeley used to have," said the girl.

"He wasn't a friend of mine," said Taxi.

He stepped into the room, feeling her critical eye on him. She wanted to see if the dead man's room would have any effect on him, and he could have laughed to think that such a little thing might trouble his expression. No, not even the dead body of Feeley would trouble him. Nothing would trouble him. He was not such a fool.

"This is all right," said Taxi.

He put down his suitcase and turned to her with his smile. He had worked on that smile. It meant nothing to him. But he could turn it on and off like a light. But it did things to other people. It made men call him a good fellow. It made women trust him. Sometimes it made them more than trust him. So he turned the smile loose on Sally Creighton. He thought that this might be a good spot to make use of it.

She was leaning against the door jamb, staring at him. Her eyes were so wide that something seemed to be pouring out of her, and through that wideness he could look at something—her soul, her mind—and he guessed that she was in some sort of trouble.

She stretched one arm straight above her to cushion her weight as she leaned against the door. Women when they're playing "vamp" parts on the stage like to stand like that, but this girl was not playing a vamp. She was just being natural. Her loose sleeve fell down. Her forearm was brown as her face. Her upper arm was white. He could see the blue of a vein in it. It was round, and so white that it looked cold. So she leaned like that against the door jamb and stared at him.

"You're going to try to get even for Joe Feeley," she said. "And you know it!"

"Why," said Taxi, "Feeley's nothing to me. Not a great deal. He's just the friend of a friend of mine. A fellow called Dell Simpson, out in Chicago. He's a broker, and he happened to ask me to find out about things when I came this way."

Taxi gave the girl his smile again, and he could see it hit her. She was not so simple as some women are. Most women are pretty simple. They haven't a great deal of sense. They're soft and sort of wide open. She was not so soft, but he could see his smile hit her. Her eyes began to sorrow over him a little.

"You can lie about what you want to do here in Horseshoe Flat," she said, "but you're on the wrong foot. What *do* you want to do in Horseshoe Flat?"

He turned a little from her and waved his hand toward the great outdoors beyond the windows. There was a fenced field beside the boarding house, and in that field stood a great chestnut stallion, bright as gold, with four silk stockings on its legs, four black silk stockings. The horse looked as though it could move, all right. It looked good enough to carry Taxi's money in almost any race.

Taxi waved beyond the horse, toward the mountains.

"I haven't been very well," he said, "and the doctors told me that I ought to get out into a big country, like the West, where there's plenty of pure air. So I came out here to look for a place to stay. That's all."

He was always pale, as a matter of fact, and no one could guess, to see his slenderness in clothes, how he looked when stripped in the gymnasium of Paddy Dennis. A good many people had told him that he ought to take care of himself. They never seemed to guess that iron is only dark with paint and not of its own nature.

The girl said: "Are you rather weak?"

"I'm not very strong," said Taxi.

She picked up the suitcase and put it on a low stand, nodding as she stepped back from it.

"You can stay here if you want to," said she. "But when you tell lies, stranger, you ought to pick them better."

"Lies?" said Taxi.

He wanted to open his eyes to express hurt amazement, but it was always better not to show his pale eyes to anyone. They could be remembered too easily.

"Lies," repeated the girl sternly. "You carried that fifty-pound suitcase all the way from the station, and you're not even breathing hard. If you're weak, most people are sick in bed."

She turned her back on him and went to the door, where she turned again.

"You can stay here," she said. "But I'm going to send someone bigger than I am to talk to you. You're here to make a big play, I know. But I've told you before to keep your hands off Charlie Larue. Now I'll tell you the reason. It's because Barry Christian is behind him! Put that in your pipe and smoke it a while, will you?"

She closed the door, and Taxi looked blankly at it.

She was different. She talked in a free and easy way, and yet she was not free and easy. She could "heft" a suitcase and then make some deductions from the weight of it. She had the straight look of a man and the soft eye of a woman. She was not beautiful, but there was something about her.

Far down the hall he could hear her rap at a door. Then he made out her voice saying, rather plaintively:

"Excuse me, Mr. Silver. I'm sorry to wake you up. But I just wanted to beg you to do something for me."

Taxi heard the soft, deep rumble of a man's voice, on which a door closed to give silence. What sort of a man was asleep at the fag end of a day, almost at sunset time? What was there in this part of the world to keep a fellow up late the night before?

CHAPTER III

Advice

It was all different. You met a woman, and she talked like a man. You met a boy, and he laughed at you. Back in New York, women were not like men. And they didn't stand around like vamps, except when they were on the stage. They didn't talk so easily. They didn't talk as though a stranger were a brother of whom they were a little tired.

He stood at the window and told himself, slowly, that

perhaps there had been some excuse for poor dead Joe Feeley if he had been interested in this girl.

Had she said that she was sorry about his death? No, she had not even said that, as he remembered. She simply had said that Larue had started drinking. A nice way to run a place—when a man starts to drink and simply rounds off the party by killing another man.

There was a gentle rap at the door.

"Come in," he called.

He was on edge, ready for anything, because he had not heard a footfall come down the hallway. The knob of the door turned without making a click. The door opened, and on the threshold stood a big man who might have been anything between twenty-five and thirty-five. He had a big head and a big, brown, handsome face. He looked like a wrestler or a heavyweight boxer from the waist up and like a runner from the hips down. Above his temples there were two queer little spots of gray hair that looked almost like a pair of horns beginning to grow from his head. He had a quiet smile and a pair of quiet, steady eyes. But those gray bits of hair that looked like horns gave him a sinister touch, as though he were a devil in the making.

He came in and held out his hand.

"My name is Silver," he said.

Taxi took the hand.

"My name is Taxi Ivors," he answered. "Sit down?"

Silver shook his head. He sat on the sill of the open window, instead, then seemed to recall himself with a start and hastily moved to the opposite wall of the room.

He was big and he weighed a lot, but his step was not a noise. It was only a pressure on the floor. Yet he wore boots, and, although on the heels of the boots there were no spurs, to be sure, such high heels ought to have made a good deal of noise on the bare wood of the floor.

"Sally—that's the girl who runs this place," said Silver, "asked me to drop in and tell you something."

"She has an idea," said Taxi, "that I'm here to go gunning for Charlie Larue. She's all wrong."

"Is she?" said Silver.

His eyes fastened on the face of Taxi. It was not a long look, but it took hold of Taxi like a hand, and he felt the tug of it. His own pale eyes opened wide against his will.

He looked aside hastily.

"She's all wrong," said Taxi. "I'm only here because I want to look up some things for a friend of mine."

"And you're trying to find a health resort, too, she tells me," said Silver.

He was smiling. There was something about his smile that made Taxi want to smile, too. There was a reassuring geniality about it. It met one like the grip of a friendly hand, and hung on, and kept hanging on. Not even a child would mind being understood and smiled at by this big fellow.

"I've got to build myself up a little, the doctors say," said Taxi.

He saw the glance of Silver take hold of him and probe and weigh him as though he were stripped in the gymnasium. Suddenly, fervently, Taxi hoped that all the men out here in the West were not like this—that Charlie Larue, above all, was not like Silver.

"This is a good place to build yourself up," said Silver. "But only if you've got the right sort of a constitution to stand the air. The air here is bad for a lot of people. It was bad for your friend Feeley, for instance. Excuse me— I forgot that he's not your friend."

Taxi said nothing. It seemed to him a good time to say nothing at all, so he smiled a little and kept his lips sealed.

The big man went on talking. He said: "I'm going to give you some information, in case it might be useful. You know Barry Christian?"

"No," said Taxi. "Wait a minute!"

For his mind was catching at something vague, nebulous, distant. It *was* a name that he had heard before the girl used it. Somewhere in the back of his brain he knew about that name.

"Prison break," said Taxi suddenly.

"That's it," said Silver. "And a lot of other things. Nobody knows the story of Barry Christian, but everybody knows enough about it to fill a book. Christian is one of those fellows who knows how to make other people work for him. You understand? Charlie Larue, for instance. works for Barry Christian."

Taxi listened, with his eyes veiled, but he kept wanting to look up and meet the frankness of this big stranger.

Silver went on: "We don't know where Barry Chrisian is. But we know where a good many of his men are. We never can hang anything on them. Not very often, that is. But we have an idea about who are the men of Barry Christian. He's so big, Ivors, that a great many fairly honest fellows are not ashamed to work for him. He sticks by his friends. When one of his men is caught by trouble, Christian opens his purse wide.

"If you touch one of Christian's men, you touch the body of a giant. The whole body turns on you—that is to say, the whole of Christian's gang. And you can't tell where you'll find his friends. Your bartender may be on the pay roll of Christian. The ranch you stop at overnight may be owned by a fellow in Christian's pay. The fellow you hire to punch cows may be a Christian man. Barry Christian has his hand everywhere, and the first thing we learn is to fight shy of a man who belongs to Christian."

He paused, and then added: "This may mean nothing to you, Ivors. But, just in case you want to tell the mutual friend of you and Mr. Joe Feeley, you might write to him that it's a good idea to keep hands off Charlie Larue."

"Thanks," said Taxi. He added: "No matter whether you're right or wrong about what I have on my mind, I'm thanking you."

He followed another impulse which seldom came to him. He stepped up close and gripped the hand of Silver. He lifted his head, and looked with his pale hazel eyes straight into the hazel eyes of Silver.

"And where do you stand about Christian?" he asked.

"I'm different," said Silver. "Barry Christian is my hobby. Every man has to have a hobby, you know."

On that speech, he left the room, and as the door closed noiselessly behind him, Taxi was willing to wager a great deal of money that Barry Christian would have preferred to be anything in this world other than the hobby of Mr. Silver.

Taxi lay down on the bed. He could think better when he was lying down. He folded his hands under his head and put his mind on the task before him. The job he had come out to do had seemed very simple. He was merely going to kill a man named Charlie Larue. Now the job seemed to be expanding. It was growing large like the mountains around him.

He got up from the bed and went to sit on the window sill and look at the golden horse that grazed in the near-by field.

As he sat in the window, he could hear beneath him, very dimly, the murmur of the girl's voice, saying:

"I don't care. He may be what you say. But I don't care how much of a fighting man he is—I don't want him to come to any trouble on account of his friendship for Joe Feeley. I was at the bottom of what happened to poor Joe Feeley. Mr. Silver, I'm going to beg you to do something."

"I'll do whatever I can," said Silver.

"Then— Oh, I know that your hands are full. I know that you're after Barry Christian. Everybody knows that. I know that you're in danger of your life every minute. But please keep an eye on the stranger. Or else I'll have his death laid at my door."

Taxi had to lean out from the window to hear what followed. He could barely hear the voice of Silver saying:

"Well, I'll take care of him if I can."

Taxi stood up. He wanted to laugh. It struck him as almost the most amusing thing that he had ever heard—that somebody should try to take care of him!

There were other things for him to think about, however. Most people, at first sight, took him for a harmless fellow, but this man Silver had apparently seen that he was a fighting man. Of that fighting man he had consented to take care.

This was a thing to be heard but not to be believed.

Then, looking out the window, as he heard a sharp whistle, Taxi saw the golden stallion gallop to the fence, where Silver waited for him. He saw the hand of the master sleek the shining throat of the horse. He saw the stallion nosing at the pockets of the man. And it seemed to Taxi that the two of them, in the suggestion of strength and speed and exhaustless power, were of a type—that he should have known beforehand that they fitted together to make a unit.

CHAPTER IV

The Round-up Bar

THERE were not many occasions when Taxi had to spend time thinking, unless it were some such problem as to how to crack a safe or get at an enemy. The values in his accepted world were fixed, and men were known by what they contributed. All policemen were "hard" or "crooked"; all women were "soft"; all children were "worthless and useless"; and, as for men, they were all on the "make."

Joe Feeley was a little different. If one had asked Taxi why he had come out West to avenge the death of Feeley, he would have been hard put to it to answer. He would have said, perhaps, that there was something about Feeley. Just something about him. That was all. He had a good grin. He knew how to tell a story. He wasn't a welsher.

But it would hardly have occurred to Taxi to call Feeley a friend. That word was an abstraction to be found in books but not in life, so far as he was concerned. Life was steel, and the "wise guy" was the fellow who had a diamond-drill point that would cut the steel of existence and open a way through it.

So Taxi, after he had reflected for a few moments, discarded the first wild flights of his fancy about big Silver, and decided that Silver was on the "make."

Now that he had decided this, he was much more at ease, for there had been beating in on the verge of his mind the suspicion that, after all, there were men of another type in the world, men who would do something for nothing, men to whom words like loyalty, and kindness, and decency had a meaning far more concrete than anything else that could be named. If that were true, then it was also true that Taxi had spent the twenty-two complicated and crowded years of his life in a perfectly futile pursuit of goals which had no real value. For what did mere hard cash and underworld fame count against the possibilities of affection and a cleanliness of soul such as he had guessed at in Silver?

Because it would have meant this denial of all value to his years of life, his years of prison and reform school, Taxi cast the thought over his shoulder. Finally, what he could remember best about Silver was the pale glimmer of his eyes and the soundless pressure of his step on the floor. This memory assured him that Silver was, like himself, a beast of prey. The memory comforted him.

"A big smart mug putting something over on me, is all," said Taxi to himself.

He opened his suitcase and put some clothes into the bureau drawers. That suitcase was packed with exquisite precision and neatness. It was always put up the same way. In the dark, his hands could go instantly to anything in it.

Now he opened a cunningly concealed false top and took out a small burglar's kit. The tools were fragile to the eye, delicate, but they were of a surprising strength. Steel tubing has almost the strength of steel bars—that was one explanation of its power. And the metal itself was of the most exquisite temper.

The manufacturer of those goods put them into the hands of only a few famous and expert criminals in various parts of the world. Each set cost a small fortune; and that manufacturer equipped his favored men with the means of taking several millions of dollars out of circulation every year. The bits of his drills cut through armorplate steel as though it were butter, and his picklock set was as supple as sword blades and as strong as hope.

All the larger tools were jointed so that they could be taken apart. Taxi was taking them apart, jointing them again, with absent movements of his supple hands, as he worked over the set. He loved every bit of it. It was like an extension of his own flesh. He had nerves in the tips of the picklocks. He had nerves in the heads of the drills. The little flashlight, hardly larger than a fountain pen but capable of throwing a sharply concentrated light for hours, was to Taxi as part of his thinking brain, its sword slash through the dark had opened for him the way through so many familiar dangers. It was his fourth set; the police had grabbed three others; and this fourth set was a little smaller, lighter, stronger than any other he had ever possessed.

He began to put away the tools. They fitted into odd places. Small mouths opened in the seams of his clothes, and into them lengths were slipped. The heels of his shoes screwed off, revealing little hollows into which various bits were put. In a moment his set was out of sight, but when he shook himself, nothing jingled. There was hardly a thing to be felt by the touch of any but the most cunning hand and the forewarned brain. And yet there were few banks in the world that would have dared to turn him loose against their thickest sets of bars and locks for half an hour undisturbed.

He felt better when he had the tools on his person. He always felt better when they were in his clothes. He was complete. Walls and locks could not hold him, now.

The room was darkening as he finished. He went to the window and saw through the dusk the strange sight of Silver playing with the stallion a sort of wild game of hide and seek in the field behind the house, sloping off toward the brook. Silver was dodging through the brush; the horse like a beast of prey was after him. It was an exciting pursuit. They were both cats, one on two legs and one on four.

No matter how the man dodged on the ground like a bat through the air, he was overtaken suddenly. The great horse reared. A cruel smile came on the lips of Taxi as he watched. And then—by magic the man was on the back of the horse, and the stallion was sweeping away with great, rejoicing strides that lifted it from the ground like the beat of wings.

Taxi kept on smiling. The cruelty was gone from his face.

"There's something in that bird," he said to himself. "Maybe—"

He shut the rest of that supposition out of his mind and went out to find supper. He could eat in the boarding house, of course, but the smell of cookery in the hall was not to his taste, which was always a little finicky. So he went up through the barren, open flats of the town to find a restaurant.

A boy with bare legs and trousers ragged about the knees began to walk a block behind him, turned when he turned, and went past the lunch counter which Taxi stopped at.

Even a boy can shadow a man, and Taxi knew that he had been followed and spotted down. But that was all right. It made him feel at home. It gave him an appetite for the food which he ordered. It kept him smiling down at his plate while, with uncounted side glances, he made himself aware of all that passed on the sidewalk in front of the big glass window, and every opening of the back door. At no moment was he more than a tenth of a second away from readiness to whip out his guns. He ate with his left hand, entirely, an art which he had learned and always practiced—because one never can tell.

One thing amused and entertained him and that was the increasing possibilities which he found in Horseshoe Flat. It looked like nothing but a naked junk heap to the casual eye, but there was life in the heap. There was life that had a poison tooth, perhaps.

After his supper, he wanted to find Charlie Larue who, according to fact, had killed Joe Feeley and who, it appeared, was under the protection of the gang of Barry Christian.

He could remember more about Barry Christian now. Barry Christian was one of those Western master minds of the criminal world who find their way even onto the front pages of Eastern journals. Barry Christian, he could now remember, was a fellow who had stood at the top of his profession in the West and whose capture had caused a stir only less than his escape from prison.

Well, it seemed to Taxi in a sense a pitiful thing that he and Barry Christian could not be useful to one another, in place of being at swords' points because Taxi had to kill a member of the gang. What was the life of an unknown man, a Charlie Larue, compared to the benefits which two master crooks could confer upon one another?

He was thinking of this when he paid his bill. There were two sections of the mind in Taxi. With one section he could observe everything that happened near by. With the other section he could carry on his own reflections and observations. The separation of the faculties had cost him much effort and training. But then he had had ten years in which he could devote himself to the training of faculties—ten years of graduate and postgraduate work in reform schools and prisons where the active mind can learn so much.

He knew half a dozen tapping codes. He knew three or four sign languages in which he could talk almost as rapidly as he could by word of mouth. He had evolved a system of gymnastics which worked every muscle of the body, so that he could keep fit even when loaded with chains in "solitary." But above all he had trained his mind to be an instrument supple, dexterous, and strong. He used to feel that his wits matched his burglar kit, and his burglar kit matched his wits.

Taxi next stopped at a clothing store and selected a wide-brimmed Stetson and a pair of boots. He had felt his own hat inadequate as a shield from the power of the Western sun, and, also, its very insignificance had seemed to make him conspicuous. For the men he saw, whatever their clothes might be, all wore hats of considerable dimensions. As for the boots, he knew that he would have some riding to do and that he would need them.

He then went up the street until, behind the flare of a gasoline street lamp, he observed the big painted sign, "Round-up Bar."

That was where Joe Feeley had been shot to death casually in this cheerful little town of Horseshoe Flat. Perhaps that same town would be just as cheerful when it wakened one morning and discovered Charlie Larue, in his turn, had died of self-defense!

He pushed open the swing doors. With his first half step through the opening he saw everything. That was one thing almost above all else that he had trained his eye to do—to glance at the wall of a cell and be able to turn away and give the sum of the number of stones in that wall. To saunter by a shop window and state, afterward, every article that was in it. With two glances, he would be able to give a very fair résumé of the chief exhibits even in the crowded windows of a pawnbroker's shop.

So, with his first half step through the swing doors, he saw everything worth noting and a lot that didn't matter. The saloon was one big room, half-divided by an open partition into a front and a back room. In the front room there was no one. In the back room two men were playing cards by a dim spot of lamplight. In that first half step, he saw both the sawdust on the floor, the places where the feet of the players had swept the floor naked, and also the nature of the game. They were playing seven-up.

He saw the bartender, too, with a fat paunch which he countered in weight by leaning so as to put a sway in his back. The man had pouched, weary eyes. He was one of those men who remain a "good fellow" until fifty and then suddenly die. A cold turns into pneumonia. Any way you take it, you can't beat the game in the long run.

That was what Larrigan had said to Taxi. "Salt Creek for you, kid. You like to see 'em drop. You like it too damn well."

Taxi always smiled when he thought of Larrigan, but his smile was half in earnest, too.

He went up to the bar and nodded to the bartender and asked for a beer. It was bad beer. It was thin and not bitter enough, and there was no head on it. But Taxi never made complaints in barrooms. He went off to a table and sipped his beer and smoked cigarettes.

He thought of a way of amusing himself. He went back to the bar and asked the bartender to show him how to roll a cigarette. The barman grinned, got a little sack of tobacco with a stiff paper label on it, and rolled a cigarette. His fingers moved like a flash. He held the thin tissue of the wheat-straw paper as a hollow trough. He sifted the yellow dust of tobacco into it. He closed the trough, getting one lip of the paper under the other. With a twist, he rolled the cigarette hard, clamped one end of the paper tube flat, and put the other end in his mouth.

He lighted it and smiled wearily at Taxi through the smoke.

"Can you manage that, kid?" he asked.

Back East, nobody called Taxi "kid." Somehow they knew better. He said he would try the trick, and at the first attempt he managed it, very slowly. The barman was impressed. The second time, after that one rehearsal, Taxi twisted up that cigarette faster than ever that barman had made one in all his days. He was amazed, and then he laughed.

"Been kidding me a little, eh?"

Taxi went back to his chair. It was always a pleasure to learn something new to occupy his fingers. Now, with the sack of tobacco and the package of wheat-straw papers, he could amuse himself, seeing how thin and hard he could roll the cigarette, or how big and firm. He smoked only a few whiffs of each cigarette; the tobacco tasted thin, and sweet, and sharp. He liked it.

Then two more men came in. One of them was a squat, waddling figure. He looked heavy with fat, at first, but afterward he was seen to be weighted down with superfluous strength. He could not keep his arms close to his sides. The bulging muscles made the arms swing wide and clear. The great hands came far down toward the knees. The other fellow was middling in height. He had a sour, sallow complexion, a tinge of red in his nose, a bright, hard eye.

"You buy this round, Larue," said the short man.

CHAPTER V

The Plant

TAXI knew everything suddenly. He knew as well as if he had opened doors in the foreheads of these men and read their minds. The two fellows in the back room stopped playing their game and went up to the bar to get a drink. They should not have done that—not if they wished to make their bluff appear good. It seemed to Taxi too patent that the thing was a plant.

The boy had trailed him. These two had entered, one of them naming the man Taxi was after. And it was apparent that the people in Horseshoe Flat knew perfectly well that he was after Larue. Even the girl at the boarding house had seemed to divine it. She, no doubt, had quickly passed the word along. Or Silver had spoken. And the conversation which he had overheard between Silver and the girl—why, that was simply another part of the big plant, purposely spoken so that he might listen in to things that were untrue.

The whole picture flashed clear and true before the eyes of Taxi. And he liked it.

They had brains, these Westerners, and so did he. Wit for wit, he felt that he could match them. Only the matter of numbers was not so cheerful. Four to one. That was a heavy count. Perhaps the bartender made five.

Still, a pair of automatics can spill lead fast when an ambidexterous man is using them. The thing to do was to sit tight and drink beer—with the left hand. The bartender was setting out the drinks. He took four glasses and without moving a step, he spun them up and down the bar. Each one stopped and rocked to a standstill near one of the drinkers. Then he took out two whisky bottles and sent them spinning in the same fashion so that they found their proper halting places.

The men poured out drinks—stiff drinks.

Larue said: "Water your face, Pudge."

That was the bartender. He took half a finger in the bottom of a glass and made a face over it before it passed his lips. He stuck out his lower lip, ready to receive the liquor in his mouth.

"Here's in everybody's eyes," said Larue. "Here's to all good guys and to hell with sneaking bums and foreign hoboes!"

That was for Taxi. His pale eyes smiled behind the dark hedge of the lashes.

"Here!" said the other four, and they drank.

One of the two fellows who had been playing seven-up called for another round. All four swung into new position, waiting. The two end men, Larue and a fellow with black, glistening mustaches dripping from the corners of his mouth, rested their elbows on the bar. The other two stepped back and dropped the tips of their fingers on the bar. This made a hollow semicircle, fit for conversation.

They would talk about Taxi. He knew it. They were spoiling for trouble.

Good sense told him to get out of the place, but instinct told him that if he tried to withdraw, he would get bullets through the back. It was a tight fit. He was not afraid, he was simply stimulated to the dancing point, so that his feet would hardly keep still. It was always that way before a fight. He never expected to be killed. He had been shot so many times, however, that at the thought of guns exploding all his old wounds ached.

There was a spot on the back of his neck that started throbbing as though an iron finger were pressing there to find the life. That was where Nick Francolini had shot him the time he was left for dead—in the waters of the East River. That had cost him four months and a long hospital bill, but a little later Nick had had quite a surprise. He had looked more surprised than dead, as a matter of fact, as he lay on his back in his swell apartment with the thick Persian rug getting all soggy with blood. A girl had been screaming, all the while, in a corner of the room. The brain of Taxi began to ache a little as the memory of her screams beat into it again.

He was not afraid of dying. But it would be painful. All the thugs out this way, he knew, carried .45-caliber Colts, and soft-nosed bullets tear out your insides. They knock you down and tear hell out of you.

"Here's to you, Scotty," they were saying to the man with the black mustache.

"Here's to all good guys," said "Scotty" slowly, "and to hell with rotten punks!"

He shifted his glance and found the face of Taxi with his eyes. Taxi sipped his beer.

Words don't hurt, but Taxi had a certain code. He felt it was foolish. He *knew* it was foolish. But even from a cop he never took more than a certain amount. Words don't hurt you, but he was queer in that respect. After a couple of verbal socks, he wanted to kill the other fellow. It was just a little peculiarity of his. It made him "go crazy" just the way he went after Paddy had clouted him on the chin about six times in a row. One more remark like this and he would have to start something.

"Here's to Babe and all other good guys," said Larue.

He slapped the squat, mighty gorilla of a man on the shoulder, and the gorilla turned its brutal face and grinned.

"Here's how," said "Babe."

"I'll buy one," said the second man from the card table. He had nervous hands that were always wandering over his face or rubbing a perpetual chill out of his arms. He was thin, his hair had no color, and his eyes were as pale as straw. In a horrible, dead-faced way he was handsome. He kept smiling. His mouth was as nervous and jerky as his hands. Taxi knew all about him at the first glance. That fellow was bad news.

"We ain't in any rush, Pokey," said Larue. "Take it easy. What's the use getting boiled on the stuff that Pudge hands out in this dump? Why don't you get some decent booze in here, Pudge?"

"What's the use?" said "Pudge," smiling. "The real men don't mind much, and the other kind drink beer."

That was for Taxi again.

He smiled at his beer and straightened in his chair a little, slowly. He knew that he was going to start something. He knew that he would continue this slow motion of his body until he was standing on his feet, saying things. He was surprised and rather awed by his own knowledge of himself. Sometimes it was like that. A will inside of him took charge and carried him along, and he could only stand by and watch where it carried him.

"I'm goin' to buy a drink," the man called "Pokey" was saying. "I gotta buy a drink because I feel a drink comin' over me. Fill 'em up."

"I'm not going to have another for a minute."

"I don't care when you have it, but fill them glasses!" cried Pokey. The last three words were a yell. He stood there gripping the edge of the bar and looking with rapid movements of his head from one to the other of them. His nostrils had flared out so that the light glinted pink through the translucent flesh. Taxi knew all about Pokey, but it made him a little sick. He was bad business, Pokey was.

The others looked steadily at him; they glanced at one another; they filled their glasses.

Pudge said: "It's all right, Pokey. Don't get heated up, old horse. Everybody's goin' to drink with you—except one."

He did not laugh with his whole face, as he said this. Only his eyes laughed.

Pokey turned around like a flash. He was all whipcord. The muscles of his rage stood out in ropes along his neck, right up to the base of his jaw. It seemed unfair that there should be a tiger's strength in a thing like that.

"He'll drink, too," said Pokey. "Nobody holds out on me. *You* drink, kid!"

He pointed a swift finger at Taxi.

"Not now, Pokey," said Taxi. "I'm having a little beer. That's all. I'll drink with you later."

"You'll drink now, or I'll pour it down your throat!" yelled Pokey.

Larue broke out into laughter. But his laughter did not make him put his head back. He kept his chin down. He kept watching Taxi, and his hands were always ready.

Maybe this was a plant, too, and Pokey had been elected to bring out the Easterner, the stranger.

Then the others would step in?

Well, something had to be done. Pokey came straight for him, striding big.

"I'm not drinking with you now," said Taxi.

"You lie! You'll drink it or choke on it!" screeched Pokey.

Taxi slid out of his chair. It's an art to get out of a chair the way Taxi got out of his, with a side step that brought him to the toes of his feet, nicely balanced.

He looked at the devil in the face of the charging man. A spark leaped out of his brain, ran down his right arm, and sprang with his fist against Pokey's chin. That spark knocked the light out of Pokey's wits. His knees went to pieces. Scotty caught him as he fell backward, and leaned him against the bar. Scotty shifted the weight into the hollow of his left arm and kept his right hand free. He paid no attention to the head of Pokey that lolled on his shoulder. He simply licked his red lips with the tip of his tongue and kept watching Taxi.

CHAPTER VI

Laughing Killer

TAXI did not "go crazy." Just that one spark leaped and was delivered out of his fist into the brain of Pokey. Then he was master of himself again.

He saw that these four were as tough a lot as he had ever seen. That went for anywhere. They had brains and they had hands and they knew how to use them. Even Pokey had not come in wide open. He had used a beautiful long straight left that would have torn Taxi's head off his shoulders if it had found a mark. But even far better men than Pokey never could fathom the crooked wiles of that right hook which was partly Paddy's teaching and partly the evil genius of Taxi himself.

Now Taxi could not help wondering what manner of man Barry Christian might be, at whose feet these lesser people sat. And what manner of man, then, was that fellow Silver who made the hunting of Christian his "hobby"?

Silver had lied. That was all. Silver was probably simply another cog in the machine.

The wits of Taxi were moving so fast that he kept seeing everything. It was always like that when he came to a life-and-death moment. He saw everything. Just as he had seen every black wrinkle on the face of the East River that night when the gang left him for dead.

Now he saw the five faces clearly enough to paint them from memory afterwards. He saw the bottles and their images behind them in the long mirror. He saw the one crack in the face of the mirror. He saw the slow hand of Pudge automatically polishing the top of the bar with a stained cloth. He saw how the varnish had been worn off the bar at the inner edge.

"He seems to want some trouble," said Larue, and smiled.

He kept looking at Taxi as he smiled. And Taxi for the first time looked up with his pale, bright eyes. It was more than a smile that came over his face. It was like silent laughter which did not shake his body. He felt that he was about to die or to kill others. And that cold ecstasy always came over him, like that.

"You're out to get me, boys," he said. "Isn't that the low-down?"

"Look out the door, Babe," said Larue.

Babe went to the door and looked out into the street. Pudge threw the polishing cloth away and leaned and picked up something from the shelf under the bar. Taxi knew what it was.

"You wanted to do a good job, and so you brought down three more to help you, Larue," said Taxi. He laughed a little, making a whispering sound with his breath. "You're such a rat, Larue," he said, "that it's not going to be much fun to lay you out cold!"

He made a little gesture. He was showing his empty hand, but perhaps they would not understand the gesture. He wanted to keep the laughing madness out of his brain, but he knew that he couldn't manage that. In another moment it would take possession and then—

Well, he'd wake up in hell or a bed. Things would be a little blurred in his memory, if he were alive, and the wounds would hurt like the devil.

"Your pals may get me, afterward," said Taxi, "but you can bet on one thing. You're dead. *You* are dead, Charlie. You're in your grave. No matter what happens to me, I can get out a gun faster than any of the rest of you, and I could kill one man while I'm falling dead."

He laughed again. He heard the whispering sound of his own breath. They all had their heads down, watching him from under their brows.

"The street's clear," Babe said.

"All right, boys," said Larue. "You think I've come to get you, stranger, and I have. I'm going to do it. Right here and now. Unless you want to put up your hands and promise to be good. Then we'll take you along with us. That's our job. Not to kill you unless we have to kill you. We want to take you along. Pudge, is that back door locked?"

"Yeah," said Pudge, "it's locked, all right."

The glance of Taxi wandered carefully over the face of Larue. From the corner of his eyes he saw all the rest of them, but he chiefly fed his eyes with the sight of Larue. The man's cheeks were hollowed out, and his nose was reddened toward the tip. His eyes stuck out a little, too. A mop of black hair hung down across his forehead from under the band of his hat.

"But," said Larue, "if you think I need help to knock you over, you're a fool."

"Listen, Charlie," said Scotty. "Don't be a fool. Remember orders and don't get away from yourself."

"You leave this to me. This is my job," said Larue. His lips curled back from his teeth.

"You sneakin' fool!" he shouted at Taxi. "D'you think I ain't able to handle you?"

"Start!" said Taxi.

With that flashing double gesture he showed again that his hands were empty. To their tips, his fingers were tingling.

He waited. Charlie Larue had not moved for a gun. The others were ready, but they had not made a move, either. They were watching Taxi and keeping one eye on their leader for the evening.

What was Barry Christian like, if his servants were like this?

"Looks to me," said Pudge, "as though this hombre wanted to make a little match of it, Charlie."

"Yeah," drawled Charlie, "the fool wants to take something. Well, I don't care."

The voice of Babe boomed from the floor, as it were.

"You got different orders," said Babe. "Mind what the orders was when we left, Charlie."

"I'm goin' to blow him up," said Charlie Larue thoughtfully. "What do I care about orders? He's askin' for something, ain't he?"

"He's asking for something," said Scotty.

"Yeah," said Babe, "he's asking for something, all right."

Babe and Scotty nodded. They considered Taxi with curious eyes.

"Stand back, boys," said Larue.

They stood back. Scotty dragged the yet senseless body of Pokey for a slight distance and then dropped him with a crash on the floor.

"You're askin' for it," said Charlie Larue.

"I am," said Taxi. "You bumped off Joe Feeley and crowded a gun into his fist afterward to make it look like a square fight. But you can't do that with me. It's no good, Larue."

"Who told you that we pushed a gun into his fist afterward? Did Arizona Jim tell you that?" asked Larue.

"Who's Arizona Jim?" asked Taxi.

Pudge laughed very briefly. His eyes were so busy wavering from side to side, taking in every detail, that he had no time to laugh his fill.

"You don't know who Jim Silver is, eh?" asked Larue. "You never met him, even?" He was sneering.

"I met him once," said Taxi. "He told me nothing. I simply know that Joe Feeley would eat a whole pack of the sort of cards you boys are."

"Would he?" said Babe, and chuckled in a profound bass. "This guy is askin' for something," he added, more softly.

"I'll tell you, brother," said Larue, smiling. "Feeley was good. He made a good try. But he was slow. Matter of fact, he got his hand on his gun, but his wishbone was split before he had it out in the open. There was a a fair start in that match, too; and there's goin' to be a fair start in this one. I'm going to show you what kind of chance a dirty gunman out of the Big Noise has when he's up agin' real work. Are you ready?"

"Ready," said Taxi.

He made a gesture with his left hand.

"Get over on the same side of the room, will you? I don't want you all around me."

Deliberately Babe crossed the room with his waddling stride and stood beside Scotty.

"Stand up alongside the bar," suggested Pudge. "Then you boys'll both have the same kind of light."

There was a powerful oil lamp hanging from the ceiling just above the bar. The inside of its green shade was a highly polished reflector that threw a dazzling image on the varnish of the bar.

Charlie Larue moved backward gradually.

"Come on up," he invited.

Taxi came up.

"Look at him," said Pudge. "This hombre has been there before, and he likes it. He's a laughin' fool, and he likes it!"

"I like it," said Taxi, with that silent laughter still on his lips. "Somebody give a sign."

"I'll say 'Scat,'" said Pudge.

"That's all right," said Taxi.

"That'll do," agreed Larue.

A genial warmth spread through the very heart of Taxi. He had heard about such things in the West. Men made a point, sometimes, of fighting fair. It was not the same process of hunt, find in the dark, shoot that he had been accustomed to. In the Big Noise it was useful to kill a man; it was rarely an honor. Out here—why, a man might build a reputation with his guns!

No wonder he laughed. A sudden glory came over him. He wondered why he had never been west of the Mississippi before.

The light from above was very strong. He bent his head a little to give shadow to his eyes. Charlie Larue had bent his head, also, but the prominence of his eyes seemed to make them catch an extra portion of light.

The seconds fell on the soul now like drops of acid. Pudge must have known it because he started to talk and kept on talking.

"Take it nice and easy, boys," he said. "When I say the word, you can make your guns jump. Shoot straight, and remember that old Pudge ain't far out of the line of fire. I'm close enough to be hit by the splash of the blood, maybe. A head shot is the best trick in a game like this. Between the eyes ain't bad. A man socked through the body may still keep on shooting, if he's got the real poison in him."

Pudge was enjoying this scene. He kept turning his head from one of them to the other.

And Taxi stood there under the light, laughing. Sometimes that laughter was an audible whisper.

"He likes it!" said the Babe, from an infinite distance.

"Shut—shut up your mouths!" said Charlie Larue.

There was not a great tremor in his voice, but there was enough. Amazement and disgust poured through Taxi.

"Are you breaking up, Larue?" he asked.

The mouth of Larue opened as if to answer, but he merely licked his lips. His mouth remained open. He began to pant.

He was dead already. No man could handle a gun when his nerves were breaking up like that.

"All right, boys," said Pudge. "Now I want to tell you a last thing before—"

Even the omniscient eyes of Taxi had been fastened on the face of Larue to the exclusion of all other things, and now he guessed rather than saw a swift movement on the part of Pudge. He allowed his attention to flicker to the side and then he saw the blow coming. Pudge had taken a Colt by the barrel and swung it for the head. The iron-weighted butt was hardly a foot from Taxi's head when he saw it coming. Even then he had time partially to dodge. Instead of smashing in his temple, the blow landed higher up on his head and knocked him into darkness.

Yet, as he had promised, even while falling, his guns were in his hands. As he slued sidewise toward the floor, he fired from either gun. The left-hand bullet ripped through the ceiling. The right-hand bullet knocked the hat off the head of Charlie Larue.

But Taxi knew nothing about that. He had fired out of darkness with the last flicker of consciousness, as a man might point in the night.

CHAPTER VII

Barry Christian

TAXI came to his senses with a feeling that a tack hammer was being rapped against the base of his brain and a pair of cymbals crashed in his ears. Then he found that he was lying on his back on the floor of a wagon of some sort, jolting rapidly over an unknown road. His ankles and knees were tied together. His wrists were tied together behind his back. His weight lay on his arms, and they were numb to the shoulders. Something tickled the side of his face. It was blood that ran in a slow, tantalizing stream from a wound that was high on his head.

Above him appeared vague figures, four of them, two on the front seat and two on the rear seat. A chain jingled continually. It ran from his neck to the wrist of one of the men on the rear seat. The driver kept snapping a whip, swearing at the horses. He spoke in the voice of Scotty, saying:

"Come on, Bec. Come on, Bird. Bec, climb into that collar. I'm going to tear the outside lining off you, Bird, and don't you forget it. Giddap, girls."

He kept saying these things in a soft voice. Finally a high-pitched snarl came from the rear seat; it was Pokey, saying:

"Shut up your mouth, Scotty; I'm tired of hearing you yap at the plugs. Leave 'em be! Beat the devil out of 'em if you wanta. But stop yapping, will you? That doesn't matter to me."

Scotty said: "He's tired of hearing me yap, says the young man. He doesn't like the way his Uncle Scotty talks to the horses. I wonder how he'd like to hear Scotty talk to a man, eh?"

"Quit the yipping!" exclaimed the voice of Charlie Larue.

"All right, Charlie," answered Pokey, suddenly subdued.

"All right, Charlie," said Scotty soothingly.

They spoke as though to a sick child that must be handled with the most tender care. This amazed Taxi. But after a time he thought that he could understand. They had seen Charlie Larue weaken under the barroom light and the fixed stare of Taxi. They had seen him go to pieces until his mouth had fallen open and he had panted like a spent runner. They had seen his lithe, strong body begin to shudder with an ague spell. It was a great deal better to watch a man go to his death than to watch a man's self-respect and confidence die out of him like that.

Even Taxi, remembering, felt a bit sick for the sake of Larue. The whole human race was shamed when a thing like that happened. And as for Joe Feeley, he was sufficiently revenged, no doubt. No matter what deeds of heroism Larue might perform, from now on, men would never forget how, on an occasion, he had grown weak and melted away and become a shuddering girl in the face of danger. The story would be told. Wherever men heard of Larue, they would hear of the hideous ordeal under which he had weakened in the barroom back there in Horseshoe Flat. It was the sort of thing that men linger over and dwell on, because each man knows that his strength is no greater than that of his nerves.

Thinking of that, Taxi looked up at the figures in the rear seat, the bulky shoulders swaying against the stars. The night was clear. By the angle of the wagon bed, they were climbing a stiff slope. The horses pulled with a regular, rhythmic jerk, keeping step, taking the buckboard haltingly along behind them. They already had gone up to a considerable height, because the air was sweet, crisp and cold, and heavily perfumed with the smell of the pine trees.

Taxi told himself that he was about to die. That didn't matter so much. He had spent most of his years in the expectation of death at any moment—except during the times when he was in prison. He had one very ardent wish before the final blow should be struck. He wanted to see Barry Christian who was the master of these four strong men.

Four stronger ones, in a group, Taxi felt that he had never met in one encounter. Even Charlie Larue was strong—perhaps there was more steel in him than in any of the others. Taxi wondered if Charlie would have been the first to weaken if it had not been that the laughing madness had come upon Taxi and perhaps made him seem more demon than man. Besides, the light had shone at a troublesome angle into the prominent eyes of Charlie Larue. Perhaps the angle of that light was sufficient to account for the way his nerves had gone to pieces. People are like that. They'll stand a lot of rubbing, but finally with one touch the fine tissue of the soul gives way and lets the darkness enter.

Some one called out. Scotty halted the horses.

"It's all right, Bud. I'm Scotty."

"I hear you say it," said "Bud" gruffly. "Flash a light on your face."

A ray of light bent across the night in a swift arc.

"All right," said the voice of Bud.

Scotty started the horses on again. One wheel, going over a high bump, rolled Taxi on his side, and he felt in the seam pockets of his coat some of the narrow tubings of his burglar set. He was amazed. He was almost more amazed than delighted to think that these clever fellows had not been able to find the tools of his trade on his person.

But, after all, a man finds only what he expects to find. That's always the way. These people probably had not heard anything about his past record. They had taken the guns away from him and they thought that was the end of his equipment, just as it would be the end of theirs. Perhaps they had felt for a knife and found none and considered the necessity of their search at an end.

Now they climbed down from the seats.

Only Pokey remained. His high, sharp voice said: "Hey, wake up!" And he kicked Taxi in the head.

The blow fell right on his fresh scalp wound. The pain made him hold his breath for an instant. Then he was able to say calmly:

"I'm awake, Pokey."

"Sit up, then," said Pokey. "Tryin' to delay the game?"

He caught Taxi by the hair of the head and jerked him into a sitting posture.

"Use your legs. Climb down out of this!" said Pokey.

Taxi rose to his feet by a difficult act of balancing.

"Now jump down," commanded Pokey.

Taxi jumped. He managed to clear the side of the buckboard and the wheels, but then of course he fell helplessly forward on his face. Luckily he had dropped on grass.

Pokey was laughing. His laughter was high-pitched and long-drawn. It sounded like the neighing of a horse at a little distance.

He got hold of the hair of Taxi's head again.

"Somebody take his feet," said Pokey.

"I'll do it," said Scotty. "Lay off him a little, Pokey. He ain't a dog; he's two parts man, anyway."

"Shut your mouth," answered Pokey. "Don't try to tell me how to handle him. I'm goin' to kill him! I'm goin' to eat him alive. I'm just getting a few tastes of him now."

"All right," said Scotty carelessly. "I don't care what you do. Come on!"

Charlie Larue and Babe had gone ahead. Now Taxi was carried under the sweet gloom of pine trees, with glimpses of the stars in between. A door opened. They passed into a very dimly lighted hall, and then into a big room.

Down in Horseshoe Flat the air had been hot and still. Up here the air was so cold that it touched his wound with fingers of aching ice. In the big room he heard the fluttering of flames. The place was pleasantly warmed. He saw wreathings of pipe smoke gathering toward the rafters. It was the smoke from a pipe because it was a heavier smell and not so sharp as that of cigarettes.

"Sit him up in that chair," said a deeply musical voice. "Hold on there—has he been hurt? Too bad, too bad! That's not a way to carry a man. By the hair of the head? Pokey, you're a cruel devil. Never let me see you do that! Never again."

"Sorry, chief!" said Pokey.

They sat Taxi up in a comfortable canvas chair.

By the way they had been speaking, he was reasonably

sure that he was at last in the presence of that great personage, Barry Christian. And he saw before him a man whose looks were worthy of his repute.

He was tall, well-made, with a good thickness of throat and the muscles stuffing out his coat across the breast and over the tips of the shoulders exactly as they should do in a perfect athlete. He was strong. He was very strong. There was not in him quite the suggestion of feline strength and speed that Taxi had felt about "Arizona Jim" Silver, but there was ample muscle about the man.

Yet after a glance, his body disappeared, and only the face remained, for plainly the empire of this fellow was ruled by the brain alone, rather than by hand and brain together. It was a lean, pale, handsome face. The texture and the color of the skin were that of one who leads a life sheltered from wind and rain and sun. The nostrils and mouth were very sensitive. The brow was magnificent, the eyes deeply set in big hollows. And this handsome face, this face that had the sensitive beauty of an artist's, was framed by a soft flow of hair that was worn long.

He wore a long brown smoking jacket of velvet. A heavy cord of braided silk was tied loosely around it. The broad collar fell wide on his shoulders. His feet were incased in slippers of soft red morocco. He looked, in short, like some landscape painter, say, who had retired to the mountains to find the scenes he loved to put on canvas. But Taxi knew that he was in the presence of one of the great criminal minds of the world.

CHAPTER VIII

Questions

CHRISTIAN seemed greatly perturbed by the ragged scalp wound on the side of his prisoner's head. He sent for hot water and bandages, at once. While he waited for them to come, he had the hands of Taxi freed from the ropes, and the other ropes were cut away from his knees and feet. Pokey sat near by with a sawed-off shotgun across his knees. That weapon was enough to take the place of all the ropes and chains in the world, when it came to keeping a man in place.

Christian filled a curved pipe and lighted it with a coal from the fire. It was a thing worth watching, to see the way in which his long, delicate fingers handled the coal, lightly, surely, putting it on the tobacco for a moment and then casting it away.

Then he stood in front of the fire, teetering back and forth, shaking his head with a frown of mute concern as he looked at the bleeding head of Taxi.

It was a log cabin, Taxi saw, but well built, with thick walls. On the floor and covering a couch were a number of the big goatskins that Mexicans love to have around. There was nothing else worth comment, except a well-filled shelf of books. Christian had been reading in a big easy chair near the fireplace; the book now lay face down on the arm of the chair.

A Chinaman came in, his pigtail bobbing with haste, and put a basin of steaming water and a roll of bandage on the table. Christian himself took charge of the bathing and the bandaging. His touch was softer than the touch of a woman. He moved without haste, but always with surety.

When, at last, he had the bandage fitted well in place, he stepped back and regarded his work with a critical eye, as though the appearance of the bandage meant a great deal to him.

"Is that comfortable?" he asked.

"It's right enough," said Taxi.

"Good!" said Christian. "Have a drink?"

"No."

"No drink? After that blow on the head and a long, cold ride in the night? Your hands are still blue!"

"I'm all right," said Taxi.

"No drinking, except with old friends, eh?" Christian smiled. "Well, I don't blame you. If a man can be sure of his company when he drinks, he's sure of a longer and a happier life, I dare say. However, if you don't mind, I'll help myself."

He poured some whisky into a long glass which he filled to the top with water. It made a thin drink, the color of the palest amber. Then he held up the glass toward Pokey.

"And you?" he asked.

"The devil with it," said Pokey.

At this rudeness, Christian merely shook a long, straight forefinger. He shook his head, also.

"You shouldn't hurt the feelings of people," he cautioned. "It's a sad thing that you insist on being so rough in your talk, Pokey. It keeps you from makin' friends. Some day you'll regret it!"

"Yeah?" said Pokey.

He wanted to say more. His nervous lips worked over unspoken words. His nervous fingers trembled eagerly over the lock of the shotgun. But awe of the chief kept the words unspoken.

The other men had left the room. Their voices sounded dimly in the distance. There was only Pokey with his gun, and Christian and Taxi.

"What happened, Pokey?" asked Christian. "You've had a fall or a blow, yourself."

Pokey lifted his left hand, keeping his nervous right forefinger constantly playing over the trigger of the gun, and made a stabbing gesture at Taxi.

"Ah, he did it? He struck you, Pokey?" said Christian. "Too bad!"

"He knocked me cold. He wouldn't drink with me. I went to pour the whisky down his neck. And he popped me. He socked me. He had brass knuckles on."

Taxi smiled.

"I'm afraid not," said Christian. "I'm afraid that he only hit you with his bare hand, because I see a slightly discolored place just below his knuckles. I'm afraid that there was nothing but muscle in that punch, Pokey. And let me suggest something to you. When you size up a man, don't go by his inches or his weight. Look not at the top of his neck but at the base of it. Look at his wrist to see whether it is flat or rounded. In spite of trousers, one can generally tell how a man is muscled about the knees. And if you note a few of these points in our friend, you'll observe that he's a very strong fellow. Very strong, indeed."

He nodded at Pokey, who merely grunted.

"And after he knocked you down—then there was a brawl?" asked Christian.

"He gave Larue some jaw. That was all. He and Larue jawed each other. They stood up to the bar. They were going to pass at their guns when Pudge gave the word. And this here, he stood there and laughed. He seemed to like it."

"Ah, well, and perhaps he did," said Christian. "We all have our little peculiarities of taste, you know, Pokey. Our friend laughed. But Larue, perhaps, didn't laugh?"

"Larue went rotten. He went bust. His mouth come open. He panted. He begun to look sick."

"Too bad! Too bad!" said Barry Christian. He made a clucking sound of regret.

"That's the great trouble with your optimistic type of man," said Christian, continuing to shake his head. "The poor fellows are very good in the quick emergencies, but when there is a long strain, they're very apt to buckle up. I'm sorry to hear this about poor Charlie Larue. It will put him on the path to murder, I'm afraid, to make his reputation good again. And finally, Pokey?"

"Well, finally Pudge saw that Charlie Larue was done in. And Pudge leaned across the bar and slogged this gent, and he dropped. As he was dropping—as he was out, complete—he gets out a pair of automatics and shoots a bullet through the ceiling, and with the other slug out of the right-hand gun, he knocks off Charlie's hat."

Just before he fell?" asked Christian.

"No, as he was falling."

"Pokey," said Barry Christian in a tone of gentle reproach, "you don't mean that as he was falling, he shot the hat off the head of Charlie Larue? You mean, as he was falling senseless?"

"I ain't talking for the fun of hearing myself talk," said Pokey. "Take it or leave it. I don't care."

"There you are again," said Christian. "Rough talk from a rough tongue. It makes trouble, and never accomplishes any good, my friend. I'm sorry to hear you talk like this."

He turned back to Taxi.

Pokey was saying: "Pudge meant to bash his head in. But the kid found time to duck even when they wasn't any time. Pudge almost missed him. Just clinked the gun on him along the top of the head. You can see for yourself."

"A well-trained fellow," said Barry Christian, shining his eyes at Taxi, "is a pleasure to meet. A man with hand and eye working together and a quick wit and a strong body and exhaustless nerve. It's a happiness for me to be with you, my friend. Won't you tell me your name?"

"Taxi is as good as any," he answered.

"Taxi? That will do. Taxi, because you run up high charges in a short time? Is that the reason that you were called that name?"

"Quite possibly," said Taxi with a smile.

"Maybe he's taken a few of the gents in the Big Noise for a ride," suggested Pokey.

"Why, perhaps he has," said Barry Christian. "My name is Barry Christian, as you doubtless may have heard my men say. I understand your reasons for not wishing to give your own full name, but though I usually keep my own in the background, I feel that this is an occasion when I can afford to talk frankly. Shall I tell you why?"

"Go ahead," said Taxi.

"Because I think," said Christian, "that either you and I will reach an agreement or else we shall have to part company. Part company," he went on in his soft, gentle, regretful voice, "in such a way that you will be leaving, at the same time, all of your old companions. You will be deserting the world you know for the unknown world. I'm sorry to say this to you, Taxi."

The smooth and profound hypocrisy of the man enchanted Taxi. He studied the fine lines of that face with a renewed interest. In most criminals there is some telltale mark of weakness. There was no such mark about Barry Christian. Instead, he seemed strong at every point.

Taxi translated the last speech: "I talk, or you bump me off."

Christian made a broad gesture as though putting those brutal words far away from him, yet he said:

"Now that you understand me, Taxi, please tell he what you're doing in this part of the world."

"Joe Feeley was a pal of mine," said Taxi. He considered the face of Barry Christian and told himself that he would speak the entire truth. To attempt to fence with this man would be insanity.

"And Feeley met with an unfortunate accident, and therefore you came out West to look into the matter?"

"That's it," said Taxi. "I got off the train, went to the newspaper office, looked up an old file, and found out that the name of the man who killed Feeley was Charlie Larue. I found out that Feeley had died of what they call self-defense, around here. I thought that probably Charlie Larue might die of the same sort of disease. I went to the Roundup Bar. You know the rest."

"A simple story," said Barry Christian in his tenderest accents. "A plain, straightforward, simple tale. Don't you think so, Pokey?"

"Oh, hell!" said Pokey.

"Well," went on Christian, "you also went to a boarding house run by a charming girl—Sally Creighton. There you met another man. Did you not?"

"I met a fellow called Jim Silver."

"In brief, what did he talk to you about?"

"He told me to watch my step."

"That was all?"

"That was all," said Taxi.

He did not need to make up his mind not to repeat the other things which Silver had revealed to him—such things as that Christian was his "hobby," and that he, Silver, intended to take care of Taxi.

However formidable a man he might be, however filled with cunning, certainly he had failed lamentably in his promise of protection! But that was all part of the game, no doubt. Perhaps Silver and Christian worked hand in glove, no matter what had been said. Yet it was also possible that Silver had meant what he said. And because of that possibility the creed of Taxi made it impossible for him to repeat a single incriminating thing about the man.

"Now, as a matter of fact," said Christian, "isn't it

true that you knew what had brought Feeley to this part of the world?"

"No," said Taxi.

Christian smiled. "Isn't it true," said he, "that you knew what Feeley had in hand and that you were determined to take a share after his death?"

"No," said Taxi.

"Isn't it true that Jim Silver had sent for you?"

"No," said Taxi.

Christian shook his head as he responded: "I'm sorry that you talk in this manner, my friend. I'm very sorry, because it might bring you to a great deal of trouble. You understand?"

Taxi nodded. He sat straighter in his chair and lifted the dark lids and looked with his pale, bright eyes straight into the mind of Christian. There he saw, behind the velvet manner, a soul as cold as a stone, a will as relentless as steel.

"I entreat you," said Christian, "not to be obdurate. I beg you to believe that you are in a very considerable danger at this moment."

Taxi smiled. His bright eyes would not leave the face of Christian.

"Very well," said Christian. He hesitated, considered his victim. Then, in his turn, he smiled. A sharp-eyed devil looked out of his face.

"Call Babe," he said.

Pokey got up with a jump. His laughter, like the neighing of a rather distant horse, filled the room.

"That's the idea, chief," said he.

He flung the door open and called. A heavy voice rumbled in answer. Babe entered the room. Taxi, without turning his head, recognized the weight and drag of that waddling step.

Christian said: "You used to be able to break a neck, Babe. What about trying the old trick?"

CHAPTER IX

Taxi's Failure

CHRISTIAN, standing before the fireplace, took the pipe from his teeth and ran a hand through his hair. It stood up high and wild, as though a wind had struck it. A passion of expectant delight was surging in him, making his body quiver. Pokey, crouched over his shotgun, made a sound every time he drew in a breath.

Then a pair of great, hairy hands were passed under the pits of the arms of Taxi. They swayed up and joined behind his head.

"Fast or slow?" asked the voice of Babe, at the rear of Taxi.

"Why—slow, I should say," answered Christian.

"All right," said Babe.

He put on pressure. The force of the leverage of the full nelson dragged Taxi's head down. He was strong enough in the neck. "A man that ain't got a tough neck can't take a tough punch," Paddy was always saying. But, though he resisted, he could not prevent the irresistible pressure on the back of his head.

"Well, Taxi?" asked Christian.

"No!" said Taxi.

He could see only the floor. He felt that his spinal column would snap in an instant. Red-hot shooting pains thrust up the back of his neck and into his brain. There were dull explosions in his ears.

"Tough, ain't he?" said the admiring voice of Babe. "Real tough. So tough that I'd like to try my hand at softening him up a little. What say, chief?"

"Soften him up? Do you think that you could soften him up, Babe?" asked Christian.

Some of the frightful strain was taken off the head

of Taxi. He became aware that he was breathing for the first time in many seconds. The breathing hurt his lungs.

"Yeah, and *I'll* soften him, too!" yelled Pokey suddenly.

"Shut up, Pokey," urged Babe. "Look at, chief. I ain't had a hand in for a long time. That back room is made to order. I'll soften him up. It'll be a cinch. I'll soften him up so's he'll talk his heart right out, in a day or two."

"There's a chance that Jim Silver will find his trail," said Christian. "There's a chance that we'd better be leaving this house now."

"If Silver comes—look," said Babe. "Is there anything better than that? We're ready for him, and he comes. He's bound to come some day, ain't he? And can he come when we're any better ready for him than we are now?"

"In your own simple, honest way," said Christian, "you have ability to go straight to the point, Babe. I have an idea that you may be right. And—do you think you'd really enjoy yourself with Taxi?"

"Enjoy myself?" said Babe. "Say, when have I had my hand in? When have I had it in for a year, pretty near?"

"True," said Christian gently. "And hunting dogs should be fed plenty of red meat."

"Yeah, lemme have him," said Babe. "I'll spread him out thin and make him last."

"Why, have it your own way, Babe," said Christian.

"Hi!" grunted Babe, delighted.

He took his hands from the head of Taxi. But he let his grasp fall on one of Taxi's shoulders, the big, blunt fingers feeling through the flesh toward the bone with a bruising and yet a merely exploratory force.

"He's the right sort, this bird. He's fleshed up right," said Babe.

Christian raised one finger.

"Mind you, Babe," said he, "if Taxi should by any chance get away, nothing will help you."

"Get away?" shouted Babe, filling his throat with laughter. "Why, after I've had him for a coupla hours, he won't be able to walk!"

"Well, well, well," murmured Christian. "Do as you please. And when you think that you've softened him enough, you can call me, and I'll have a look at him."

"It won't be long," said Babe. "I know a coupla things, chief."

He lifted Taxi to his feet and took him with a prodigious hand by the nape of the neck.

"Walk, son," said Babe.

He took Taxi into a hallway, down it, and through a door into a small room. Taxi made no effort to escape, partly because he knew that if he made a sudden lunge, that one hand might almost break his neck; partly he was quiet because he knew that Pokey was following, carrying a lantern and holding the sawed-off shotgun under his right arm. Only the rankest fools in the world take chances when there is a sawed-off shotgun in the field against them.

Pokey hung the lantern on a peg in the wall.

There was nothing in the room except a wooden cot with a pair of blankets thrown across the canvas.

"Lemme stay and look," said Pokey, leering.

"You get out," answered Babe.

Pokey left, cursing his luck. "I'm goin' to have a crack at what you leave of him, one day," said Pokey, as he went out.

"Yeah," answered Babe. "Maybe the buzzards are goin' to have their chance at this hombre."

He locked the door behind Pokey and put the key in his trousers pocket.

Taxi, seeing all of that room at a glance, saw that there was nothing that could in the least degree serve him as a weapon—nothing except a leg of the cot, if he had a chance to pull it off.

If he could get at the lantern and put it out, then in the darkness that ensued, he might be able to do something with this man beast. But he was by no means sure.

He had been at a zoo and seen an orang-utan smile, the lips wrinkling back, fold after fold, until the big canines were exposed. Babe was smiling at him the same way now. His mouth was a huge slit, but the lips were much larger than they needed to be. They were thin, and they had to pucker up in the center so that they would fit with some closeness over the teeth. And the teeth themselves, at the corners of the mouth, were extra long and extra sharp.

Taxi realized, with a sense of curious surety, that this

man could hardly be blamed for anything he did with his life. There was not room for a proper brain under that cramped forehead. The back of the head actually sloped forward from the bulge of the vast neck. There was very little to the neck. Taxi felt that if he tried for a flying stranglehold a mere lowering of the vast, craggy chin would break his arm.

However, the strongest rocks may be split if they are tapped at the proper place. The proper place to tap the human rock is just beside the point of the chin.

"All right," said the brute. "Take off your coat, kid. I don't want no padding on you when I start patting you."

Taxi slid obediently out of his coat, seeing that his jailer was also peeling off a coat and exposing a shirt of thick red flannel. It was a perfect opportunity. Taxi spun suddenly to give the full weight to his punch. He took a flying hitch step forward and slammed his right fist, like a lump of iron, right on the button.

The shock started his arm trembling to the shoulder. The shudder of that vibration went right through his body.

It was his right hook delivered as he never had sent it home before. Paddy had said that even a giant would fall if that punch landed fairly on the button, but surety must be made extra sure.

The delivery of the blow had swung him off to the left, leaning forward. Now, as he straightened himself, he swayed all his weight, all his lifting power, all his savage despair, into two driving uppercuts. They landed, one, two, right under the chin of Babe, and Taxi stepped lightly back to let the ruin fall.

But Babe was not falling.

There was a red streak on the side of his chin where the force of the first blow had actually split the tough hide against the bone, but in the buried, apelike eyes of Babe there was no sign of dimness. He was smiling. He had not even continued his attempt to pull off the coat which was now wedged over his elbows.

He bobbed his vast head up and down in short nods, because his abbreviated neck did not allow him much of a sway. The bulge of his chest struck his chin too soon for that.

"Good!" said Babe. "For your weight, kid, you're a beauty."

Taxi, standing back toward the opposite wall, understood that he had failed and he knew what that failure meant.

Babe finished taking off his coat. He folded it with care. He brushed off a spot of dust that troubled his eye and laid the coat out on the cot.

After that he turned slowly toward Taxi.

His loose lips were stretching, rolling back from his teeth, closing, grinning again, just as the mouth of the orang-utan in the zoo had smiled when the keeper came, bringing fresh food.

In the mind of Taxi flashed a perfect picture of the big yellow teeth sinking into his jugular.

Then he stepped out, with a good, high guard, to fight his best—though he knew that his best would not be good enough.

CHAPTER X

Torturers

BABE could not hit Taxi. He could land on him, but never solidly. Babe tried everything he knew, and he knew a good deal. He shadow-boxed, with Taxi as the ideal target. He tried shifts and double shifts, one-two punches, overhand wallops, swinging, chops, jabs, half-arm and full-arm uppercuts. He feinted and hit; he double and triple-feinted and hit; and always he was either having his punches muffled while they were still in the air, or else Taxi rode with the blows to rob them of force.

In the meantime, Taxi was doing execution of his own. He did not hit many times, comparatively, but his strokes counted. He played on the loose lips of Babe. He played at the bony ridges which covered his eyes, and thumped him on the abortive nose which was like a shapeless lump of gristle in the middle of Babe's face. He drew streams of blood from Babe before at last the gorilla decided that man-made methods of war were not for him.

He simply waded in through Taxi's attack and crushed him to numb helplessness. Then he trussed Taxi under one enormous arm. He held Taxi close and beat him with a deliberate enjoyment with the other fist. It was like a lump of lead incased in a bit of rubber hose. Wherever it fell, it bruised. When he was satisfied with what he had done to Taxi's face, he turned him over and beat him across the kidneys and lungs. Blows there hurt ten times as much as blows struck to the head.

After a while Taxi could not move. Then Babe took him by one foot and dragged him into the big room at the front of the cabin, where Barry Christian looked up from a book.

"He can still listen to you," said Babe. "Wanta talk to him?"

"Let me have a look at him," said Christian.

Babe took up Taxi by the nape of the neck and muscled him out at arm's length. Taxi tried to stand straight, but his legs wobbled beneath him as though they were adrift in a troubled current of water. He tried to hold up his head, but Babe had beaten the base of his neck, and the nerves wouldn't work. His head fell over on his shoulder.

"Sit him down by the fire, the poor fellow," said Christian. "No, please not in that chair, Babe. We don't want the blood to stain everything, do we? Just leave him there. I don't imagine that he'll get up and run away."

Babe laughed. "He won't run away," he said. "I done it scientific. He won't get up and run away."

Taxi looked at him. He could almost sympathize with the immense contentment of Babe.

"It looks to me," said the gentle voice of Barry Christian, "that he did a little scientific work on you, too, Babe."

"Does it?" asked the Babe cheerfully. He took a forefinger and collected the blood off his face and flicked it into the fire. Babe began to laugh. "Yeah, he's scientific. You take a little fist, like his, and it cuts, is what it does. But I never had a better time in my life. It was like shadow boxin', and the shadow couldn't be hit. It was like punchin' at a dead leaf, and the wind of your punches keeps knocking that leaf out of the way. I never had a better time. It was exercise, was what it was."

"A little more exercise like that, and perhaps you won't have much of a face left," suggested Christian.

"Well," said the Babe, "the good thing about a mug like mine is that it'll stand wear. It ain't pretty but it'll stand wear. I'll plant a beefsteak on it after a while, and it'll be all right. Maybe Scotty will have to take a couple of stitches over this here eye. I don't know. If you got some good material, it'll stand patches."

"Get some vinegar," said Barry Christian.

"Not for me," said Babe.

"Get some vinegar," said Christian.

Babe went for some vinegar and came back with a glass half-filled with it.

"That's all the chink says that he can spare," observed Babe.

Christian held the glass in his hand and closed his eyes as he inhaled the strong fumes.

"Now, Taxi," said he, "can you talk?"

"Yes," said Taxi.

"Perhaps you've observed," said Christian, "that we are people who mean what we say. For my part, I've allowed this to be done with regret. A quick and merciful killing would have served my end, but Babe thought that he could soften you a little, to use his exact words, which you'll remember hearing. Therefore I've allowed him to try his hand. And after all, Taxi, isn't it better for us to endure a little pain on earth than for us to rush straight into hellfire? Or will you go to a pleasanter place?"

Taxi smiled.

"A sense of humor, too," said Christian. "And what could be better than that? What could be more humanly useful? It proves that a man has capacities for tact and contact, humanly speaking, when he shows a sense of humor. I hope you will prove to have sufficient sense, Taxi, to understand by this time that it would be much wiser for you to talk to me?"

"Well?" said Taxi.

"I mean to say, it would be wiser for you to tell me what I want to know—why Silver asked you to come out here and what Silver has in mind to do. What clews he picked up about—well, let's call it about Feeley's little game. Are you ready to talk?"

It seemed to Taxi a fortunate thing that this was a subject on which he did not need to make a decision. The decision was already made by that code according to which he had to live or die. The code says that a man in the final pinch does not talk. He takes his medicine and does not talk because talking eventually turns a man into something worse than a dog.

"No," said Taxi. "I'm not talking."

"Listen to him," said the Babe, with enthusiasm. "He's all right, ain't he? He can take it. He likes to take it, I tell you."

Christian sighed, rose from his chair, and leaning over Taxi, began to separate with his fingers the lips of the wounds on Taxi's face. Into those wounds he poured vinegar. The effect was incredible. In each case it was like having the flesh seared with red-hot iron.

One groan swelled the throat of Taxi and could hardly be stifled. After that his swiftly-working brain paralyzed his entire body. It takes practice and a will of steel to be able to do that. But when one knows that the other gang is about to take possession of one's body, it is well to will the body out of existence. That was what Taxi had learned to do. He had gone through the third degree half a dozen times, also, at the hands of those earnest inquirers, the police. Therefore there was very little about the enduring pain that he did not understand

With all the might of his brain he gripped himself, numbed himself, and withstood this torture.

Finally Christian stepped back. His nostrils were quivering as though he were inhaling a delicious fragrance. His eyes shone with the light that Taxi had seen in them once before.

"Look at that bird!" said the Babe. "Can he take it? He can!"

"There remain the eyes," said Christian.

"Yeah. There's still the eyes," agreed Taxi.

"And you're not talking?" urged Christian.

"No."

Christian leaned over him once more. He plucked up

the swollen lid and allowed the vinegar to run in on the tender ball of the eye. The burning seemed to pass right on into the center of the brain. It seemed to eat away at the very core of that nerve power which had been ruling out the sensation of pain. One great shudder ran through the body of Taxi. He told himself that he was about to scream out. And then, by the grace of mercy, he fainted.

When he recovered, he was lying on a damp, cold floor of beaten earth. The lantern on the wall burned obscurely through the mist in the air that was half water vapor and half smoke.

He could see that through the slits that remained to him. It seemed strange that there was still the power of sight in his eyes. But he could see the smoking light of the lantern, and he could also see the face of Babe, who sat in a chair at a side of the room. There was no window. There was a short flight of steps leading up to a door which was flush, at the top, with the ceiling. Some small buckskin sacks were piled in the corner of the room. There was nothing else to see. Gradually he understood that he was in a cellar beneath the cabin.

He pushed himself to a sitting posture. His wrists were manacled behind his back. His legs were manacled at the knees and the ankles. His coat lay beside him on the ground.

Babe now looked up from his newspaper. He sat slued to the side in order to bring his paper into a better relation with the lantern light. Now he folded the paper and turned his battered face toward Taxi.

"How feeling, boy?" he asked.

"Fit as a fiddle," said Taxi weakly.

"That's good," said the Babe. He asked anxiously: "Feeling like talking yet?"

"No," said Taxi.

Babe sighed with relief. "I knew you wouldn't," he remarked, almost fondly. "I had a kind of a faith and a trust in you, like a baby. I knew that you wouldn't buckle and knuckle under like a cur. There's stuff in you, kid, that I been countin' on. I suppose we better take our little exercise. Kind of just a matter of form that I had to ask you, first, if you wanted to talk."

He came to Taxi and lifted him from the ground and

beat him, holding him with one hand, hammering him with the other.

On every bruised place Babe's fists fell with a redoubled force. The whole nervous system seemed to have been multiplied by a thousand in order to register the force of that agony. The weight of the blows drove out the breath in gasps, whistling through the clenched teeth of Taxi. But those breaths never became vocal.

After a while he knew that his senses were fading out of him. He felt that another endurance test, like this, would be the end of life in his body. Then the lantern light began to darken and ceased.

When he wakened again, he was alone in darkness. He told himself, at first, that he was simply blind, but when he spoke the name of Babe, he received no answer. He was actually alone. In addition, he felt that he was dying.

Thirst was a greater pain than the bruises which covered his body. Besides, he lay in a stinging fire of fever that consumed him.

After a while, he found that he was breathing more easily. He began to forget all the pains in his body as he concentrated on the faces of these men. He called up Barry Christian, Babe, Larue, Pudge, Scotty, Pokey. He called them up as judge and as executioner. He began to apportion deaths for them.

So it was that after a time he found that his own pains were disappearing. If he allowed his mind to turn to them, the agony rushed back over his brain in a wave. So he calmly turned his mind from the pain, and therefore it was no more.

They had left him in darkness, trusting to the irons and the effects of the beatings that had stretched him senseless to keep him quiet. Nobody in the know back East would have been so foolish, but of course these fellows could not understand what he was able to do.

He started to slip the cuff off his left hand. That was why he went, each day, through exercises which made that left hand supple. It was a painful job, but he knew all about the pain. He could draw the hand through the steel grip for a little distance, but then it stuck. And now he found that his strength was so limited that after each effort the dizzy sickness spread over his mind again.

He had to relax and devote his attention to deep breathing. Then pain would leap at him and have to be ruled away. When that was gone, he would try again. Finally he got his left hand free. The skin on the backs of the knuckles and the thumb was scraped away, but that made no difference. His left hand was free!

Next, he sat up. It was not easy. His arms were strong, but his back seemed to have been broken. Every time he stirred, he discovered that the wave of agony swept him to the verge of the abyss of darkness. So he had to handle himself very daintily.

He was a brain with a pair of able hands. He had no body at all; he had no legs, either. Babe had attended to that. Babe was thorough.

First Taxi got out the slender pencil of his flashlight and cut the darkness with the ray. In an instant he had seen all that was present.

Then he took out a picklock and almost in three touches he solved the three locks which held him. He was free—except for the weights and chains which the torture laid upon him.

CHAPTER XI

Raw Gold

CRAWLING was hard. Rolling was much better, except that half of it which brought his back against the ground. With greater and greater frequency he was threatened with fainting spells. Each time he found himself lying on his face he paused to breathe a while.

When he came to the heap of little buckskin sacks, he indulged in another moment of rest, which he employed by making his hands fumble at the sacks. They were filled with something loose but so heavy that it was very hard and compact. He unknotted the ear of one sack and onto the ground poured out a stream of the contents. He put the spot of light from the torch on it and saw that it was a current of gold dust, still ebbing out rapidly. It built a glistening pyramid that pushed its head against the open place in the sack; then the fine dust ran no more.

It seemed to Taxi that everything was explained now. Where there is raw gold, men will become beasts. These fellows in the cabin were all animals because under their feet was a treasure. Mere blood is nothing. The sight of it may make a sensitive fellow a bit sick. But the sight of gold will make the same man into a ravening mad dog.

Taxi smiled, and then he went on until he was at the foot of the steps. He could not roll up them, of course. He had to lay hold on the steps one by one with his hands and edge himself higher and higher. He could only move his body with a slight serpentine wriggling in order to help his arm power. And each time he planted his chin on a higher step, he shut his bruised, burning eyes and breathed again.

When he got to the top of the stairs, there was a shallow landing. He lay there for a long time, breathing, waiting. After that, he was able to reach the knob of the door and with an effort pull himself to his knees.

Then all the strength seemed to go out of his arms. A shuddering fit of weakness threatened to let him fall. That, however, he endured.

He got out the picklock again, and worked with it in the lock. He felt almost a touch of regret as he solved the thing. It was strange that a great man such as Barry Christian should trust to such simple locks. But even the greatest of us have our weak or our careless moments.

The door pressed open. A hand from without seemed to be working it. Then he realized that it was the hand of the wind. The sweet, pure air entered his body and gave him a new soul. The old one blew away and a confident, more living soul was in him.

High above, he could see the bright glittering of the stars, dancing with the eternal life. On this dark, low earth we cannot hide our actions.

There were more steps to climb now. He went up them in the same manner, using his chin as a pry against his weight, pulling with his arms, wriggling his body a little, snakelike.

And so he came to the top and lay among leaves and pine needles that had drifted over the surface of the ground.

Out of the night the rows of big pines seemed to be slowly crowding toward him, saying: "We will shield you from observation."

He had been wrong, he decided, about open country. Wherever there are men, there is pain to endure; only in the open country can one find the gentleness of nature and the peace. As for himself, he had lived among men as a wolf lives among sheep. That was the only reason why they had seemed necessary to him.

Now he could work his body sidewise and commenced the rolling. Gradually he hitched around and started turning himself. It was not so painful, out here. The needles that cushioned the ground gave him ease. He had gone perhaps ten turns of his body. He was almost among the trees when a door of the house slammed and a great ocean of lantern light began to sweep across the ground. It came in waves, measured out by the beat of the steps of the man who carried the lantern—a low, squat man. That was Babe!

He went straight on to the head of the cellar steps, humming in the depths of his throat. Then, with a shout, he whirled about. He came straight at Taxi and flopped him on his back. Taxi closed his eyes against the agony of that sudden turn. But, instantly mastering that weakness, he smiled straight up into the eyes of the giant.

"By the dear old hind hinges of hell's gate," said Babe, greatly moved.

He raised his voice to a thunderous roar.

"Hey! Come on!" he yelled. "Hey, everybody come out! Everybody come on out! You hobos, come out here and see a gent that has a brain in his head."

Pokey got there first, racing like a greyhound. He leaned over Taxi and cursed with wonder. The others came streaming after.

"You seen him," said Babe, making a speech of a sort of proud despair. "You seen that he couldn't walk. He can't walk now. He can't even crawl. He can only snake along. But he takes off three sets of the irons and he opens the locked door and he comes up here to take a little crawl and get the air. A kind of a constitutional was what he wanted. He sort of needed to work up an appetite, I guess. Now, you gents seen him before and right here you can see him this minute. If anybody told me this, I'd bust him on the jaw and call him a liar."

He took Taxi by one foot and dragged him back to the head of the cellar stairs. He jerked him to his feet and swung back one ponderous fist.

"Get back where you belong!" said Babe, and smashed Taxi in the face with his full force.

The blow picked Taxi off his feet, hurled him backward. He struck on the steps below. A great red flame burst up before his mind. Then he lay at peace, perfectly still.

CHAPTER XII

Two Strange Things

JIM SILVER, leaving the boarding house, had merely said to Sally Creighton: "You can't tell. He's late, but he looks to me like the sort of fellow who may enjoy late hours."

She shrugged her shoulders and kept her troubled eyes on him.

"I don't know, Mr. Silver," she said. "I only know that I'm terribly worried. He's not like other people around here. He's more like Joe Feeley."

Silver nodded and went out to look. The first place he looked in was the Round-up Bar, because he knew certain features of its repute. There was no one in it except Pudge, the veteran bartender.

He nodded his head and made his puffed, debauched eyes smile.

"Evening, Silver!" he said. "Step right in and have one on the house."

"Thanks," said Silver.

He took one finger of whisky and drank it slowly. The first taste was a critical one, to determine the possible presence of unknown substances in the drink. He finished and nodded to Pudge.

"Have a round on me," he invited.

"I don't mind if I do," said Pudge.

So the glasses were filled again.

"I'm looking for a fellow who may have been in here this evening," said Silver. "About five ten. Slim-looking. Eastern style. Pale. Black hair."

"Haven't seen him," said Pudge. "Hold on a minute. Yes, I guess he was in here for a minute. Had a glass of beer."

"That's right," agreed Silver. "Beer is probably what he would drink. He didn't have the whisky eyes. When did he go out?"

"I wasn't looking at the clock," said the bartender. "A while back, was all."

"Anybody with him?"

"Not when he come in."

"But when he went out?"

"Yeah. He'd hitched onto a party of two or three. Three there was."

"Who were they?"

"I didn't place 'em," said Pudge. "All strangers to me, they looked like. Big fat feller was one of 'em. He was talking about traps and bounties and cursing his luck this season. I guess he was a trapper, all right. There was one they called 'Texas,' too. Had a star embroidered on the tops of his boots. And another was an old hand. About fifty, I'd say. Grizzled, kind of. Sort of down on their luck, all three of 'em looked like to me."

"Three of them, eh?" said Silver. "Heeled?"

"Heeled? Nothing on the outside, but they sort of *looked* heeled, if you know what I mean."

"What were they talking about?"

"A game. I didn't hear everything they talked about. The gent you're after don't talk up very loud and bold. And you notice where there's one gent talks soft, it tames down the others, too."

"It does," agreed Silver. "They talked as though they were going off to start a game of cards, did they?"

"That's what they talked like."

"Hm-m-m," said Silver to the bar, rubbing the tips of his fingers over the smooth varnish. "Cards? Cards?"

In the profundity of his thought, as he tried to fit card playing into his optical and mental picture of the stranger, he lifted his head and looked toward the ceiling.

"Hello!" said he. "Somebody been shooting up the place?"

He pointed to a hole in the ceiling's plaster.

Pudge turned suddenly about. With his back to Silver, he bent his head until his fat red neck formed a dozen deep wrinkles above his collar.

"Oh, that?" asked Pudge, pointing in turn.

He turned around and faced Silver.

"That was weeks ago," said Pudge. "That crazy gent, Larue, was in here. He's always pulling a gun and doing tricks when they ain't wanted. He gets to doing a double roll, and a gun goes off and I'm glad to tell it didn't nick anything but the ceiling."

"How long ago?"

"Oh, I dunno. A long spell back. That Larue is a tough hombre, Silver."

Pudge leaned a little across the bar, glanced toward the swing doors, and then lowered his voice to confidential tones.

"A gent like Larue is poison to a bartender, Silver. Plain poison. He's a bad one to have around. I don't dare to throw him out, but havin' him do his drinkin' here turns a terrible lot of people away from my bar. Peaceable gents don't like to have a wild cat like that rubbin' elbows with 'em alongside a bar."

"True," said Silver. "They don't like it, and a lot of them won't have it."

He turned and regarded, for the first time, a small dark spot on the floor. He rubbed it with his toe, and the spot spread a little.

"Blood on the floor, Pudge," said he.

"Blood?" said Pudge, starting a little. His eyes grew very wide and round. Then he added: "How did that happen? Oh, sure. That gent—that grizzled old one—he gets a nosebleed, a regular spouter. Consumption, or something like that, I'd say. By the caved-in look of his chest, consumption, I'd say."

"Would you?" said Silver, smiling.

The bartender regarded the smile and frowned. "Why, yes," he said, "I'd call it the con. What would you call it?"

"Bunk," said Silver.

"Hold on, Silver. I don't foller your drift," said Pudge.

"Why, there are a lot of queer things," said Silver, "around your bar to-night. There's blood that can fall all the way from a man's nose and hit the floor without spattering. And there's a bullet hole in the ceiling that still leaks a few grains of plaster from time to time, even though it was made three weeks ago. Two strange things, I'd say!"

Pudge grew, gradually, the deepest of crimsons. He dropped his head a little and began to polish the bar with a cloth which he picked up from the shelf beneath it.

"There might even," said Silver, "be a little pile of plaster on the floor under that hole in the ceiling. Mind if I take a look behind the bar?"

"I do mind," growled Pudge. "The public ain't welcome behind my bar, Silver."

"Never make any exceptions?" asked Silver.

Pudge put back his towel beneath the bar. His hands remained out of sight.

"I don't make no exceptions," said Pudge slowly. "Not even for a Silver."

So Silver dropped his left hand lightly on the edge of the bar, and his right hand, with a light gesture, picked a Colt from beneath his coat. There were four extra inches on the long barrel of that gun, and yet it was as a feather in the practiced grasp of Silver.

"Whatcha want?" asked Pudge, as the white came into his face in streaks, to take the place of the red.

"I want you to back up," said Silver. "Back up slowly, Pudge. Keep your hands at your sides, and back up. Move carefully. You're an old-timer around here, and you know that accidents can happen. Don't die of self-defense."

Something bumped with a metallic clank on the shelf below the bar. Gradually Pudge drew back against the row of bottles before his mirror. His hands were empty, and the fingers were twitching. His stomach worked in and out with his rapid breathing.

"This here is an outrage, Silver," he said. "You been havin' your way too long, all over the map. Maybe it's about time for you to hold up a little! Maybe you're startin' to go too fast."

"Maybe," agreed Silver, and planting his left hand again on the bar, he leaped lightly over it.

One hand of Pudge had gone out to grasp the neck of a bottle as he saw the body of Silver in the air, but observing that he was still covered by that famous long-barreled gun, he relaxed his grip again.

Silver stood before him, laughing.

"You've got the old fighting stuff in you. You've got plenty of it, Pudge," said he. "I like it, and I like you, in spots. You might hoist your hands over your head, though, while you're about it."

"A plain holdup!" exclaimed Pudge.

Silver pointed to the floor.

"You let the dust lie on the floor for several weeks, Pudge, do you?" he asked, pointing to a scattered little heap of plaster. "You scrub up all the rest of the floor, but you leave that pile?"

He turned back on the bartender.

"And a gun under the bar, too. It's a rough town, Pudge, but not as rough as all that!"

"Your own business ought to keep your hands full," snarled Pudge. "Edge away from mine, will you?"

"I can't do it," answered Silver. "I'm sorry, Pudge, but I simply can't do it. Because I have an idea that you may know a few things that will do me good."

He picked up the Colt that lay on the shelf beneath the bar, commenting: "Good old single-action, with a filed-off trigger, eh? Didn't know that you could fan a gun, Pudge!"

Pudge swore fervently.

"And here," said Silver, "is something that looks as though you brushed your hair with the butt of this gun. Hold on, though. It's not the color of your hair. It's black!"

He pushed the gun slowly onto the bar. His face had turned rigid with anger. His eyes, for the moment, burned as pale and as bright as the fighting eyes of Taxi.

"The bit of hair that's caught on the butt of your gun, Pudge," said he, "would fit in with the hair on the head of Taxi, that Easterner I'm looking for. Know that?"

Pudge growled: "Is there only one man in the world that has black hair?"

"You hit Taxi with that gun," said Silver. "I've almost a mind to hit you with mine, Pudge. You're fat, and you're old, but even rats get gray and puffy, sometimes. And I've an idea that you're a rat."

Pudge said nothing. It was not a time for speech, and he knew it.

"You hit Taxi. And then some people took him away. Was Charlie Larue in the party?"

The hit made Pudge wince a little. He moistened his lips and shook his head.

"No," he said.

"You lie," said Silver. "Larue *was* in the gang. Who else?"

"I don't know," said Pudge.

"That blood on the floor came from Taxi, did it?"

"I don't know," said Pudge.

"Was he killed?"

"I don't know," said Pudge.

Silver drew in a breath quick and deep.

"If you were only ten years younger, Pudge—" He sighed.

He vaulted over the bar again. Pudge stood with his hands still above his head.

Silver turned and walked deliberately toward the door. The gun of Pudge lay right before him on the bar, and still he failed to lower a hand and grab at it.

Not until the swing doors had closed behind Silver did he bring down his hands.

There was a high stool behind the bar, and onto this he slumped. The starch had gone out of him. There were no muscles in his back. He folded his hands on the bar and dropped his forehead on his hands. His shoulders heaved with his breathing.

Silver, when he reached the street, glanced up and down the wide, empty thoroughfare. It was probably useless for him to ask questions. Besides, he knew that it was the work of Barry Christian's men. If Larue was in the game, then Christian had a hand in it, and that meant that the disappearance of Taxi was simply another act in the long drama of Silver's fight with the great outlaw.

He looked helplessly around him at the mighty sweep of the mountains against the stars. Barry Christian was not far away. He was reasonably sure of that. When men like Larue and Pokey and others of celebrity remained near the town, it was most highly probable that the great Barry Christian was himself close at hand. But in the great forests, in the rock nests of the higher mountains, in the entanglement of ravines that split the upper slopes, whole armies could be hidden. It was a true hole-in-the-wall country; that was one reason why Barry Christian was favoring it with his presence.

Silver went back to the boarding house and found that his hostess was in the kitchen.

She had finished washing the dishes. Now she was scrubbing out baking tins and frying pans, using sand soap and a heavy brush and a great deal of elbow grease.

Silver took a chair, leaned back against the wall, and surveyed her.

"Talk or work," said the girl. "Don't just sit around and be the big chief."

"I'll talk," said Silver. "You sit down over there and talk, too."

She turned around suddenly.

"I'd rather stand," she said. "Have you found out anything at all? Has anything happened to him?"

"Sit down," commanded Silver.

She sat down on a stool near the stove. Her eyes opened at him. Suddenly she became like a child. But the anger in Silver was too profound for him to have pity.

"He's blotted out—for the time being. Maybe for good and all," he said.

She squinted her eyes shut. She gripped her hands suddenly together and shook them hard.

"I knew it!" she muttered. "I was sure, I was sure! I felt that something had happened to him!"

"He went into the Round-up Bar. Pudge knocked him out with the butt of a revolver. Larue was in the party.

And now Taxi has disappeared. You have a right to know that. There are some other things. There was shooting in the Round-up Bar, this evening. I don't know why there should have been shooting when the butt of a gun had already done the work. But I'll find out other things later on. What I want now is information from you."

She kept her eyes closed, and since they were closed, she was swaying a little on the stool.

"What's this Taxi Ivors to you?" snapped Silver.

"Nothing. I never saw him before to-day."

"What's Taxi to you?" he insisted.

"Oh," she cried out, "he's a lot. I never met any one like him. There *is* no one like him."

"Is he a fast worker?" asked Silver.

"He didn't look at me, he didn't lift his eyes."

"That's because he has eyes that can be too easily remembered," said Silver. "But if he means something to you, we'll get on better. I have an idea that it wasn't murder. I don't know why I feel so sure. Barry Christian's men don't tap their victims over the head unless they want to take them alive. If they've taken him alive, he may soon wish himself dead. Unless we can find him. But you'll be able to help me."

"I?" said the girl. "Then tell me how!"

"By telling me about yourself and Joe Feeley," said Silver.

"There's nothing to tell you," said the girl.

He shook his head.

"You'll have to talk out if you want to help," he observed.

"I'll tell you anything," she said.

"Were you fond of Feeley?"

"No. I liked him. He was jolly. I wasn't fond of him."

"Was Feeley fond of you?"

"Yes."

"You're sure of that, and what makes you so sure?"

She hesitated, then crossed the kitchen, opened a cupboard, and from the far corner of a shelf she took out a handkerchief which she unknotted.

"He gave me this," she said, and poured into the palm of Silver's hand a small, gleaming heap of gold dust.

CHAPTER XIII

Reading Sign

SILVER took some of that shimmering dust and sifted it through his fingers. The girl lifted her eyes to his face. He stood back.

"Well?" he demanded sternly. "Where did he get it?"

"He didn't tell me. Somewhere in the hills. Somewhere near his cabin, I suppose."

"Cabin? Did he have a cabin?"

"There's an old shanty up yonder in the hills. I can show you where. He used to go up there every second day and look around for deer. He never shot a deer. He was no good with a rifle. He told me that he was born with an automatic in his fingers but that he never had worked much with a rifle. He couldn't hit a deer. But one day he came back here looking scared. He showed me some gold dust in the palm of his hand. 'I've found it in the ground!' he said. He was wild with excitement. I asked him if it were real gold. He said he didn't know but that he'd see if it were good enough to buy a drink with. So he went downtown."

Silver nodded. "That's what killed him, then," he declared. "When Feeley paid with gold dust, like a fool, the whisper about it came to Christian. He put his men on Feeley's trail. They found the place where the gold was washed. When Feeley came back to town, they followed him down and killed him so that he couldn't go back to his diggings. I don't suppose there's any doubt about that. It was after the first time that Feeley brought you this gold?"

"It was the next evening. He went down to the saloon, the Round-up Bar, and Pudge took the dust in payment for drinks, all right. Joe Feeley was half-crazy, when he came back and told me that. He said that he was going to wash a cool million out of the ground and marry me, and all that sort of thing. He was crazy."

"What about you?" asked Silver.

She shook her head. "Gold is catching," she said. "I was excited, too. I went to the dance with him in a fever. But I knew all the time that I didn't want to marry him. After the dance, that night, he wouldn't wait for the morning. He rolled his blanket and went off in the dark to get back to his cabin. I asked him where the place was where he'd found gold.

"He liked me, all right, but he didn't like me well enough to tell me that. He only laughed. 'You don't care about the place,' he said. 'All you'll need to care about is the gold that comes out of it. I'm going to buy you. I'm going to put you in one side of a scales and weigh you down with gold that I stack in the other side. Understand that?' That's the way he was talking. He was on fire. He told me that money wasn't money, unless it came out of the ground. He said that it was dirty stuff and there was murder on every penny of it, except what came out of the ground."

"Poor Feeley," said Silver. "I'm sorry about him. If I only knew where that claim is—well, I'd be able to find some of Christian's men there, I suppose. And if I could find the men, I could trail them home, and if I trailed them home, I'd be fairly close to Taxi—if he's still above ground. Sally, come out and point the way for me. I'm going up to that shanty."

"It'll be hard to find the place where he washed the gold, though," said the girl. "I've been up there three times, since poor Joe was killed. I know the lie of the land, up there, and I've searched everywhere. I couldn't find a trace."

She put the gold into the handkerchief, knotted it, and offered it to Silver.

"Take it," she said. "I don't want it around me. Whenever I see it on the shelf, I think of poor Joe Feeley's face laughing and wrinkling up to the eyes. He was hard as steel, but he was a good fellow."

Silver made a gesture as though to refuse that gift, but presently he changed his mind and without a word dropped it into his pocket.

Parade took him swiftly over the flat of the Horseshoe plain and up the slope of the mountain. There were seventeen hands of Parade, but the wild years when he had run free, leading a herd, had made him as wise-footed as a mountain goat. He knew by a glance the rocks that would slide under foot and those which would remain firm. He knew how to zigzag up the steepest slopes and just that throw of the foot, coming downhill, which puts the frog of the hoof against slippery ground. He needed all of these arts before he brought Jim Silver to the cabin.

It was hardly worthy of the name. It was a mere lean-to that was propped against a rocky bank and it was made of a queer mixture of sapling poles and logs and thatch. Time had broken and warped and thinned it until the eye could glance out of it in almost any direction.

Silver, standing on the floor of beaten earth, took heed of the bunk that was built against the wall, the fireplace of blackened stones that stood in front of the door, the homemade stool, the table made by stretching across a pair of large stones two logs which had been flattened by ax work. That was about all there was to see.

There was a slight natural clearing in front of the shanty, and the pine trees shouldered up in close ranks all around this open place. The ground was rather rocky and thickly covered, in most places, by pine needles. There could hardly have been more unfavorable land for trailing, but that was what Silver had to do. Somewhere, from this starting point, one of the trails which Joe Feeley had made led to his gold strike. That trail Silver was determined to find.

He disregarded the immediate vicinity of the cabin but entering the trees, he laid out several large circles which cut across semiclearings in the woods, where the soft soil would take and hold the print of feet. After a time he began to locate trails that went out and in.

As for those which went out from the cabin, they made a hopeless proposition, because it seemed that Feeley, like the usual hunter, never went out in a fixed direction but left his cabin and rambled wherever fancy led him. It was plain that Silver could work for months on those signs without reaching a definite conclusion to his labor. The incoming trails, however, were more promising.

Two or three of them, to be sure, clambered up the mountains from lower ground, but the majority came in from above. And the strongest and freshest of the trails, as Silver made out after careful study, raking away pine needles, comparing sign for sign, had been covered a number of times. It might be that this was the trail from the gold strike.

In that case, it was rather strange that there were not tracks both incoming and outgoing. Since only incoming marks were visible, it might be that Feeley, fearing he might be observed, on each occasion had left his house and gone to his mine by a circuitous route. However, having arrived at the diggings and worked them, he probably had come back in a more or less straight line.

One thing was fairly certain. From the rounded nature of the little nuggets in that bit of gold which Silver was carrying, it was reasonably sure that the metal was water-washed and shaped. Therefore he could look for some water-course, not necessarily a new one, but perhaps some dry old bed from which the stream had been turned in the process of time.

Almost every step was a difficult one and meant dropping on his knees, often, to make sure of the impressions which he sought after. Sometimes, where there was a soft undermold and only a thin layer of pine needles on top, he scraped away the needles and found beneath them the sign he was looking for. He made ten failures for one success, but the successes eventually enabled him to chart a line, and the line of course gave him a direction.

It was laborious work but it was exciting, too. The sun was very strong, but there were blowing clouds, high up, and when they crossed the sun, a wave of cool shadow washed across the mountain and left Silver in a dull twilight. But the next moment there would be sun again shining through the treetops and gleaming on the upper surfaces of the thick branches, and spilling through like sheets of gold leaf on the carpet of pine needles.

Of course the trail had variations. If it were in fact laid down by the feet of Joe Feeley, he had not taken one single route even on his return trips, but had swung to the side here and there to avoid various trees or outcroppings of rock. Silver had to put together some dozen of these different routes before, in the end, he was able to mark the signs with a multitude of little twigs. From the twigs he finally charted the eventual line which, as it seemed to him, Feeley had been walking along.

By the time he came out of the heavy press of the pines to the comparative open, he found that his line of march pointed straight at a confusion of big mountain slopes. It was close to dusk. The sun was going down and he knew that he would have to wait until the next day before he resumed his work.

He did not return to the cabin. It seemed too dangerous a business. Therefore he took Parade a hundred yards away into a clearing where some good grass was growing. He had for his supper hard-tack and water out of a runlet. Then, while it was still faintly light, he rolled himself in a blanket on a bed of heaped pine needles and went to sleep.

A pale moon looked down and wakened him once during the night. Then he slept again until the first morning light commenced. The air was almost as cold as frost, but when he got up, he stripped and washed himself at that runlet of snow water. By the time the morning gray had turned to rose and the mountains were no longer black against the sky but beginning to take on some of the dawn color, he had breakfasted on a piece of hard-tack and was back at his work.

He was disheartened when he discovered how little ground he had covered the day before. But now, calculating his line with the greatest care, he saw that it pointed straight toward a mountain with a big, round-bellied slope that poured down to the south, opposite him. He gave up that step-by-step trailing and marched straight off to make a two-mile cast ahead.

The end of his march found him on the breast of the mountain stepping over shimmering rocks without a sign of footmarks anywhere about him. Nevertheless, as the heat increased, he went over the ground inch by inch. Anything, a single impression was all that he asked for. It was nearly noon before he gave up the task.

If the rocks showed nothing, perhaps it was simply

because no foot had happened to strike on one of the few bits of soil that filled the hollows among the stones. Therefore he cast straight ahead over the mountain.

Again there was nothing before him.

Parade began to grow impatient. He had followed at the heels of his master during all of this time without finding more than a few salty shrubs to graze at. Now he started walking around and around Silver in a narrowing circle. It took a matter of life or death to close the mind of Silver to the wants of his horse, but life or death was exactly what might be in the balance now. So he went on through the fierce heat of the afternoon, rather hopelessly, because there was no sign of a watercourse before him or to either side. It seemed as if water could never have been there, but as though this terrible sun must always have dried the rocks to the core.

He stood up from the vain survey of a stretch of gravel when he heard a light rushing sound like wind in the distance. No wind came to him, however, though the sound continued. He hurried forward and found himself on the bank of a little stream that ran fast as though down a flume. There was no ravine. There were no trees to mark the course. There was simply this trench slanted across the face of the rock. And Silver felt that he had found what he wanted, at last.

CHAPTER XIV

The Placer

HE climbed down the bank and looked at the water. Everything about this creek was extraordinary, but nothing more so than the fact that the little river had been able to pick up so much mud in the course of its journey across solid rock! It should have been as limpid as crystal!

It pointed, however, straight as a rifle barrel across the slope and into the mouth of a small valley filled with stunted pines, for the elevation was great and timber line was not so very high above them. In that valley the stream might pick up soil, though it was strange that there was such variation in the degree of muddiness. As Silver watched, he saw the current run almost clear, while the next moment it was clouded brown again.

He put his hands into the wash. Something struck his fingers. He pulled up his hand with a blade of green grass laid flat across the palm.

Then he understood, and smiled. A normal stream does not eat its banks away so fast, except in floods, that the green grass is taken down the current. Up yonder in that little valley of the pines men were digging away at the soil. Men were there washing the ground for the sake of the gold that was in it. He was as sure as though he had stood on the spot and observed them bending, working the pans, spinning the water around and around in them until the sediment cleared away and the scattering of brilliant yellow remained at the bottom.

He got on Parade now, and made a detour that took him up to the head of the valley. Already the day was slipping away from him. The sun was out of sight beyond the great western mountains, and the sunset would begin to pour its dim tides among the valleys very soon. He left Parade screened from view behind a grove of young pines that were barely taller than the head of the stallion; then he went down the creek, exploring.

Its headwaters were not far above. The waters had worked out a faint depression on the shoulder of the mountain, here. Then a little runlet came in from the left with a rush that turned both currents into a shining dance of many small waves. The steady growth of the pines began here, the trees bending away from the prevailing northwestern stream of the wind. A little farther down, two more sparkling rivulets of spring water joined the main stream which now began to meander through a shallow hollow.

Voices came up to Silver from that hollow. He got down on hands and knees to worm his way through some brush, and so he came within arm's length of a man seated crosslegged on the ground with a rifle across his knees. If the fellow had not moved, Silver might not have seen him until too late.

Perhaps it was too late already!

Little by little, an inch at a time, Silver drew back. The sunset color was streaming with the clouds toward the south before he had maneuvered himself to another place where he lay out, propped on his elbows, and looked down on a busy scene. There were four laborers in the bottom of the hollow. They had stripped away the upper layer of thin turf and left bare a surface of black sand, or loam. This they were cradling, standing in the run of the water and spinning the mud out of the detritus until the small residue—Silver could guess what it was—was dumped into a common milk pail.

They finished working while Silver looked at them grimly. This was the mine that poor Feeley had discovered and for which he had died. Now, no doubt, Mr. Barry Christian was giving to his devoted followers one half of the loot while he kept the other half for himself. Perhaps he had taken a fortune out of the placer already; perhaps there were more fortunes left, though it seemed to Silver that the greatest part of the gold-bearing sand in the little valley had been already washed. It was a mere pocket of a richness at which Silver could not guess. At least Barry Christian had been willing to take a life for the sake of it; but there were varying reasons for which Christian would take life, and one of them was no more than that it satisfied his naked whim.

The old anger which had gathered in the heart of Silver so often when he so much as thought of the man returned upon him now, a dark and settled hatred.

They were ending work. The picks, shovels, and cradles were laid under a tree. The milk pail was emptied into a small-mouthed buckskin sack that had a good weight to it. It must contain, however, only what they had washed on this day.

In the meantime the riflemen from the head of the valley stood up and sauntered down to the miners. They all streamed out of the hollow and took their way on foot right across the brow of the hill.

Silver, watching them through the gathering veils of the dusk, saw them enter a deep pine wood, which extended over the head of a neighboring summit. He followed when the darkness had increased a little. From the very peak of the next hill he looked over the tips of the trees and saw what he had hoped to find, a thin drift of smoke that topped the trees and melted away toward the south in the wind. That was probably where they were camped, and that was where he must hope to find Taxi, if in fact there remained any hope of locating him.

Silver returned to the stallion. With the dusk the wind had risen, well-iced off the higher summits. He felt weak, a little feverish. He kept telling himself that he had done enough for this one day, and that a good night's rest was what he needed, after bending all those hours under the hot burden of that sun. But even while he argued against conscience, he knew that conscience would win, driving him sullenly on. For if Taxi were in fact alive in the hands of Christian's wolfish men, he had probably been through something that was almost worse than death.

He rode Parade down to the verge of the woods. There were horses not far away, when they entered the trees. He could tell that because twice Parade threw up his fine head to whinny, and he had to lean over quickly and catch the horse by the nose in order to stifle the sound.

He dismounted. Already it was the darkness of night under the pines, with the wind blowing the fragrance and with it the icy cold into his lungs. At such a time the temptation is either to surrender or else to stride blindly forward. Silver did neither. The more impatient he grew, the more he took hold of himself with a mighty grip and steadied his nerves.

There in the dark, he made himself halt, and standing perfectly still, he listened to every sound that breathed through the trees. He lay down and with his face against the ground hearkened again. He could hear nothing except the natural noises of the forest, the sound of the wind like the rushing of a great water, and the occasional deep groan of a branch against another.

He went on, often bending over. For an eye close to the ground sees all silhouettes in a clearer proportion. But he did not see the house until he was right at the edge of the clearing. Even then he could not make out the line of it clearly, for a time, as the pine trees beyond it make a background into which it faded so perfectly, and the only lights were thin slits of yellow around the well-shuttered windows. The size of the place surprised Silver, when at last he had completed a survey of it.

After that, he took Parade back into the woods and by pressing a foot behind the knee of the stallion gave him the signal to lie down. There he would remain prostrate even if a forest fire blew raging toward him. Silver turned back to prospect his find.

CHAPTER XV

A Night of Waiting

SILVER spent the majority of that night gradually freezing to stiffness and trying to get at the house. But it was a hard job. There were two men on beats, walking constantly back and forth, and each of them carried a sawed-off shotgun. Inside the clearing there would be no chance for long-range shooting, and sawed-off shotguns would be more efficient than a whole battery of rifles.

That was the Barry Christian touch, the perfect proportioning of means to ends. It seemed to Silver that he could see that handsome face, and the tall, elegant body relaxed in some easy chair near an open fire, while Christian thumbed the pages of a book, contented, or lowered the volume to see his brilliant dreams of the future build themselves in the flames of the fireplace. And that thought, like fire in the blood, sustained Jim Silver through the freezing hours of the night.

Three times he retired to a distance and ran himself warm. Three times he came back and resumed the watch. It was hopeless. He kept telling himself that and yet he kept on waiting. If Taxi had ever been there, he was probably dead long before this. Christian was unlikely to have any use for him.

Very little happened to break up the terrible monotony

of the wait. Once the kitchen door opened, and a Chinaman came out and threw a pan of dish-water far out on the ground. Silver saw the pock-marked deformity of that ugly face in profile as the man turned back toward the light.

In the deep middle of the night, two men came out, and took the places of the pair that had been standing guard. Silver, lying couched in the brush near by, heard the conversation between one pair. He who had been pacing with great strides up and down beside the house exclaimed now:

"Yeah, and I thought you'd never come. You're an hour late, Scotty."

"Steady, Pokey," said Scotty. "I'm right on the dot. Maybe five minutes late, but the Chink didn't wake me up till a minute ago. I came right out."

"It's a fool business, anyway," said Pokey. "What's the good of walkin' a man up and down till his heart freezes inside of him? I feel as if I'd swallowed a chunk of ice. And what's the good of it? I'll tell you the good. It's the way that Christian has to show us that we're the dogs and he's the driver. That's the good of it."

"Silver's on the job," said Scotty tersely, and a shudder ran through Jim Silver as he listened.

"Silver?" exclaimed Pokey. "Silver's down there in Horseshoe Flat."

"He's left the Flat," said Scotty. "We got word a while ago. It came up from Pudge. Silver has tumbled to things. He knows about all he needs to know."

"How *could* he know?" demanded Pokey.

"I don't figure that. He went in and made a play at Pudge. Silver knows that Taxi was knocked flat with the butt end of Pudge's gun, that Larue was on the job, and that a hole was shot in the ceiling. He guesses that Taxi was taken away alive by the boys. Is that enough for him to guess?"

"But how?" groaned Pokey. "How the devil could he make that out unless he threw a scare into Pudge?"

"Pudge don't scare," said Scotty. "Pudge is fat, but he don't scare. He's a fighting fool. I don't know how Silver made it all out. There's no use asking. Better ask a bloodhound how it manages to follow a trail."

"I don't understand nothing," complained Pokey. "I don't make out what Taxi is to Silver, anyway."

"Silver must have sent for him. That's all. And Silver's the sort that never lets up when a partner of his gets into a pinch. He goes through hell if he has to, but he never lets up. It's the nature of the fool."

"Aye," said Pokey. "And I hope he never gets his fool hands on me!"

He went back to the house, while Silver gritted his teeth over the news that he had heard.

Yet, as he circled cautiously around the house, wondering what chance might come to him, hour by hour there was no opening. The house was entirely dark now, and around the cabin the two guards maintained a perfect watch, striding up and down with their sawed-off shotguns ready. Not once did they pause, even to make and light a cigarette. Not even Roman sentinels could have been truer to their posts.

And then the morning began, with definite notice to Silver that the end of his vigil was approaching. He felt a shuddering sense of rage and disappointment. He could have groaned aloud.

For one thing, he had not made out from the talk of the pair even so much as whether Taxi were alive or dead, though it seemed certain from what they had said that he *had* been alive when he was taken from the Round-up Bar.

In the meantime, he could see the fellow called "Scotty" more and more clearly, as the morning light commenced. He could see the steam of his breathing, and the glistening of his long mustache, and the resolute sway of his big shoulders.

And now chance for the first time inclined to Silver, for Scotty, as the light freshened, leaned his shotgun against a tree and made a moment's pause to swing his arms and bring the blood back into warm circulation through his body.

Silver, rising as a cat rises from its long vigil beside the rat hole, slipped from behind his patch of brush to the rear of the tree. He was there as Scotty turned to pick up the shotgun. Instead, he got Silver's fist against his chin and dropped in a heap.

Silver gathered him up, propped the heavy, loose burden in his arms, and carried him swiftly back among the trees.

By the time Silver put him down with his shoulders against the roots of a big pine, Scotty was already opening his eyes and muttering. The chilly muzzle of a revolver laid under his chin, after Silver had found and taken the man's own gun, quickly restored Scotty to his full senses. He tried to sit up, realized exactly his position, and sank his big shoulders back against the roots, that projected like knees above the ground.

"Scotty," said Silver, "do you know me?"

"I never saw you before," said Scotty. "But you're Silver."

"Then you know," said Silver, "that I'm not here to waste time, brother?"

"Right," said Scotty.

"I want to know," said Silver, "whether Taxi's alive or dead."

"He—" began Scotty, and then closed his teeth with a click.

"Mind you," said Silver, "it would be a pleasure to me to lift the top off your head. Is that clear?"

Scotty locked his jaws, and said nothing.

"I count to three," said Silver, "and then Heaven help you!"

He counted slowly, and at the third count the body of Scotty stiffened, his eyes shut tight.

Silver pulled the gun away from his chin.

"All right," he said. "You win, Scotty. Only it's a pity that good stuff like you should work with Barry Christian. Roll over on your face. I'm going to tie and gag you. I won't choke you. I know how to do the trick."

Without a word, Scotty turned on his face, and Silver took out some strong twine that was always in a pocket of his clothes and tied his man securely. Scotty's own bandanna, well knotted, made a sufficient gag.

Then Silver stood up gloomily. He had secured his retreat, to be sure, but that was his total accomplishment after two long days of labor.

A voice called from the house: "Scotty! Where are you, Scotty?"

Silver stepped quietly back among the trees until he could see the face of the house once more, and beside it he observed the form of an ape-like man standing at the top of what were apparently the cellar stairs. The creature was blinking as he stared around him, as though even the light of this pale day were unaccustomed.

"Hey, Scotty!" he repeated, more loudly. "Where are you, Scotty? Ain't you goin' to bring me my coffee? Hey, Scotty! Coffee! And a shot of whisky for Taxi, will you?"

It seemed to Silver, as he heard that last word, that he was repaid for the entire length of his vigil. He kneeled behind the brush that had sheltered him before.

Just inside one of the shuttered windows he heard a voice say: "Aw, shut up and leave us sleep and go get it yourself, will you?"

The man by the cellar stairs turned and stared at the window from which the voice had come. Then he nodded and strode with a waddling step toward the rear of the house. He turned out of view around the corner.

For half a breath, Silver considered. If that voice through the shutter had come from one who had merely wakened and turned in bed, he was safe. If it came from a man on the alert behind the window, he would be running straight into the face of death. However, his hesitation endured only that instant. Then he started up and ran rapidly over the ground toward the cellar entrance.

It was wide and clear before him. There was the dark descent into the black of the underground room which was only half relieved by the light that burned down there.

He went down those steps in two bounds, and came, gun in hand, into the presence of a body that lay sprawling on the beaten earth of the floor. It was like a dead thing; it lay with body uncomposed, as a lifeless creature would fall. One blood-soiled bandage was wrapped around the head. The face was battered almost out of human shape and covered with cuts intermingling with the bruises, and crusted over with dry scabs of blood. He was able to recognize Taxi more by the slender frame of him and the shape of the head than by the features.

He gave one look upward toward the floor above which the men of Barry Christian, and perhaps Christian himself, were living. If all their lives had been in his palm then, he would have closed his grip. Then he sank to his knees and picked up the senseless man.

He treated that limp figure carelessly enough, throwing it like a half-filled sack over his shoulder. The hands of Taxi dangled lifelessly about his knees. But, held in this manner, with one arm he could manage the weight of Taxi, and with the other hand he could fight his way, if there were need.

Then he ran lightly up the cellar steps, a drawn gun ready in his grasp.

As he came up, he could see that the rose of the morning was now thoroughly staining the zenith; when he reached the open level, coming as he did out of semi-darkness, it was like issuing into the brightness of midday. The trees around the clearing seemed to be polished with dew; they shimmered softly before him. He heard, in the house, the voice of the Chinaman raised in a shrill protest, and then the laughing, booming voice of the ape man as he issued again from the house, letting a door slam behind him.

Silver was running toward the trees, as he heard this. He ventured no glance behind him, for he knew that at any instant the ape man would turn the corner of the house and see him. And the trees drew closer and closer. The green gloom of them was more than a blue heaven to Silver.

And then: "Hey! Help! Help!"

An automatic opened behind him with a rattling pur.

Another voice yelled on a shrill, echoing note: "Silver! Silver! He's here!"

A rifle struck out a more ringing, a more metallic note, and then Silver was with his burden among the trees. He was unhurt, if only that senseless body which was loosely pendant from his shoulder had not been struck!

He whistled.

Behind him, as he ran, he heard many voices shouting. He heard the squeal of a horse that was being mounted and started to a run by the cruel thrust of a spur into velvet flanks. And in front of him he heard the crashing of brush and the beating of hoofs; he saw the glimmer and then the whole body of Parade coming like a bird to the nest!

He swung his burden over that mighty back, mounted, and set Parade off at a large-striding gallop.

They broke out from the trees. Before them was the gradual and falling slope of the mountainside over which the morning was now brightening. Behind him the beating of hoofs sounded like a confused pulse in his ears. The arms and the legs of Taxi flopped up and down like the foolish, stuffed limbs of a doll. Silver cut to the left, and with one cry let Parade know that he was running for his life.

CHAPTER XVI

The Gorge

THE best course for ultimate safety was straight back through the mountains toward Horseshoe Flat. But that was a helpless and hopeless ideal of safety. There had to be considered, first of all, that one horse must carry two men. And though there were seventeen hands of Parade, though no horse in the mountains could match strides with him, even his strength could not endure that weight for long.

That was why Silver sent him slanting across the long down slope as fast as he could leg it. He could only hope to put between him and the enemy a sufficient distance, early in the race, so that he could hide from the pursuit.

And that would be like trying to hide raw meat from hunting cats.

He picked up Taxi by the middle and steadied that loose bulk before him. The head of Taxi fell back on Silver's shoulder and jounced crazily up and down, up and down. Sometimes it flopped off the support and had to be replaced.

It was no time to be nice. Silver turned his head to

the side and grasped a lock of Taxi's hair between his teeth. That steadied the bouncing of the head. He could give both hands to the support of the body. It seemed to be broken at every joint, and a terrible fury came up in Silver that made him want to turn and charge straight back into the teeth of destruction.

There came destruction itself in the form of five riders who had swept out of the woods far behind him.

They were far behind now, and they would be still farther to the rear after the stallion had maintained this pace for a few moments. For Parade, summoned by the voice that called out to him from between the teeth of his master—a deep, groaning, appealing voice—was flinging himself over the ground with the fullness of his might.

With side glances, his head turned, Silver counted again the men behind him. He who came first was that same ape man from whose immediate hands he had stolen the prisoner. Behind him at a good distance, gaining steadily because their bulk was less in the saddle, were three more. And last of all and most of all came a man who would have been by himself enough to occupy all the brains, the cunning, the experience, the fighting hands of Jim Silver.

He knew that upright carriage, that air almost of disdain, that calm indifference with which the rider was sweeping his horse over the broken ground. Even at that distance he thought that he could tell the magnificent silhouette of the head and shoulders against the rose of the morning sky. For that was Barry Christian!

He was to the rear now. There were lighter weights in front of him, far in the lead; but before the end he was sure to be in the forefront. Merely by the gigantic power of his will he would get from his horse more than any other man could summon.

Then Taxi roused from unconsciousness.

His eyes opened, and Silver saw the flash of the pale eyes, turned up toward the flames in the sky. A faint, twisting smile touched the lips. Then the eyes closed again.

They opened once more. They turned with a vague, struggling glance on Silver and remained on his face.

"Silver!" said the faint and groaning voice of Taxi.

"We're going to beat them, Taxi," said Silver.

He no longer steadied the head of Taxi by holding the lock of hair between his teeth. That head no longer joggled and bounced lifelessly, but was sustained almost steadily by the man's own strength. His body seemed a lifeless pulp, but there was life in the head and eyes. A little life in the hands, also; for now one of them gripped the back of the saddle to take some of the strain away from Silver.

Taxi looked back.

He saw, behind him, the streaming flight of the five riders in pursuit. Their yelling voices sounded in his ear like the voices of so many hawks, screaming in the sky. And he was the prey that an eagle had seized on and was bearing off toward safety.

His brain was still clouded. It had seemed to him, at first, that he was borne through a sort of cold fire, a world of cold fire. He was dead then. He was dead, and his soul was carried on rushing wings through the flames of hell. Soon they would winnow him with ethereal heat, but now they were still at a distance.

Then the agony of his body called him back to life in a realer measure. He was aware of the strong arms that upheld him. The gallop of Parade forced the cold sweetness of the morning air into his lungs. He could think, and his first thought was of what motive worked behind the brown face of his deliverer.

In the beginning all was mystery. How this one man could have entered the house of the enemy and taken a senseless body out—that was the greatest mystery of all.

Why, now, he risked his life by making his horse carry double in a race which must be lost if it endured long was another thunderstroke to the brain of Taxi.

There was some hidden reason, of course. People don't do things unless they have a reason. The preservation of his life was important in the eyes of Silver. Otherwise Silver would not be there. What that importance might be was a closed book to Taxi. But he was willing to wait for developments. There are many things in this life which cannot be solved by the first glance of the eye.

And above all that was strange was this sense of being cared for by the brain, the courage, the skill of a stranger.

There was no bond between them. They had entered into no partnership. They belonged to no "crowd."

Back in the memory of Taxi remained the words that he had overheard between Silver and the girl. Silver had said that Taxi would be his care. But it could not be that there was no profound cause for that care.

In the basement of the house of Barry Christian, there in the mountains, gold was packed in many little buckskin sacks. That, perhaps, was the reason at the base of all. Behind every mystery there is always a question of money, if you look far enough!

So these thoughts struggled through the mind of Taxi as Parade rushed him forward through the cool morning air. Sometimes his physical agony made all thoughts a blank, but he kept the screaming of his nerves far back, as a rule, buried in a corner of his consciousness. When things like this were happening, it was no time to be aware of mere bodily pain.

A ravine opened to the right.

They swept down it with a speed increased by the greater slope. It seemed impossible that the shoulders of any horse could endure the frightful strain that was falling on the forelegs of Parade. But he was all steel—all steel under a golden sheathing.

A smile came again over the face of Taxi as he muttered: "What a horse!"

Silver said nothing. He rode with the grip of his legs only, his hands and arms supporting the body of Taxi. Now and then he turned his head a little to measure the increasing distance between him and the men behind. They were yelling no longer. They were saving brains and breath for the work of jockeying their horses to a greater and a greater speed.

Now Parade swept out of the ravine into a more open valley. Silver groaned as he saw it, and Taxi could understand why.

The going underfoot was smooth enough, but the floor of the valley stretched before them endlessly without so much as a tree to give a hint of shelter. To the left there were trees enough, to be sure. There was a great wave of brush and pines that swept on up the mountain, and in which they well might hide themselves. But on the nearer side of the narrow canyon there was no more than an occasional lone tree.

"What's up?" asked Taxi.

"We're done for," said Silver through his teeth. "Parade is almost finished. There's no cover. And we can't stand off five men when one of 'em is Barry Christian."

That was simple mathematics. No, they could not stand off five men when one of them was Barry Christian!

Far behind them came the enemy, streaking. Taxi, as he glanced back, saw them waving their hats in circles, a certain sign that they considered the battle won.

Then Silver with one sharp call brought Parade to a halt, and flung himself down to the ground.

Still with his hand he supported the limp body of Taxi.

Taxi said: "Go on, you fool! Let 'em have me. You can't beat 'em. But if you're riding alone in the saddle, this pony will walk away from that crowd. Go on, Silver. I don't know what you expect to get back from me, but it's not worth the price!"

Silver made no answer. He had cut off the reins close to the head stall of the hackamore which served him instead of a bridle. Now, with the reins, he lashed the feet of Taxi beneath the belly of the stallion, and, drawing Taxi forward flat on his face, tied his hands with full force around the neck of Parade.

Next he picked up the light end of a fallen tree trunk that lay close to the verge of the little ravine. Years had stripped away its foliage. He upended it, walked it up into the air, and let it topple forward.

Crouched forward, tensc with anxiety, Taxi saw Silver standing as the trunk fell straight and true across the dozen yards that separated the walls of the little ravine. It dropped with such force that it seemed certain that the slender tip of the tree would be broken off. But there was seasoned strength in the long, fragile sapling. The tip of it recoiled and bounced up from the shock, and the long trunk lay trembling across the breach.

Taxi could understand now. It was a sort of bridge that Silver had laid down across the stream with this one swift gesture. But what living man could cross such a structure, what walker of the loose wire, even, could step across that trembling, uncertain, rolling support?

The thought of walking was not in Silver's mind, however. But, swinging out from the near side of the gorge, he grasped the round of the trunk between his hands and so carried himself on, swinging pendulous from his hands, taking one great arm haul after another like a sailor on a rope.

That was the meaning of the big shoulders, the long and powerful arms.

To the left, rushing down the valley, came the five, with big Barry Christian already in the lead and pulling a rifle out of its sheath as he saw what went on before him. To win Taxi, to win the great horse, Parade, might be something; but it was nothing compared with the loss of such a prize as Silver. That was plain.

Taxi saw that Silver was close to the farther end of the trunk. He saw the meager tip of the tree bend, sag terribly, slip away at the point where it rested on the opposite rock. And then feebly Taxi yelled the warning, and saw the tree go down. Silver disappeared.

No, it seemed as though a mysterious hand caught and buoyed him up in mid-air while the trunk leaped like a living thing into that hundred-foot abyss.

Some projecting ridge, invisible to the eyes of Taxi at that angle, had been found by the catlike feet of Silver as the man fell. Now he was swarming up the face of the rock, standing on the top of it, shouting a wild appeal to Parade.

For what? To come to him!

The breath left the body of Taxi as the great stallion came to the edge of the ravine, so that Taxi could look down into the chasm and hear and see the white frothing of the stream. It sang on a hollow note, prolonged by endless echoing.

On the verge of the gorge Parade reared. The strength of his neighing sent a great shudder through the body of Taxi. Then the big horse whirled and ran back.

With dizzy eyes, as Parade turned, Taxi saw the men of Christian racing toward him. Christian himself, well in the lead, was firing shot after shot, not attempting to level the rifle from his shoulder on that racing horse, but shooting it from the ready. How closely he was edging the target was told by the keen wasp sounds that darted by the ears of Taxi.

And now, turning back toward the gorge, Parade rushed it at full speed. He was going to try the leap. Taxi knew that. There was no more turning the massive rush of the horse than of checking a huge avalanche.

That was as good a way as any, when a man had to die. Better than the torturing hands of Babe.

Then Parade left the ground with a wrench that jerked Taxi far to the side. Along the flank of the stallion he lay bunched beside the saddle. Beneath him he saw the white of the churning water. They seemed to hang in mid-air. They dropped. The hoofs of Parade struck the rock with a force that drove Taxi almost under his belly.

The big stallion was still struggling to gain a footing on the ledge when consciousness left Taxi.

CHAPTER XVII

The Care

WHEN Taxi recovered his wits, he lay in semidarkness with a smell of moist earth strong in his nostrils. When he stirred, the voice of Silver said beside him, in a whisper:

"Be still! Don't stir! Don't breathe."

Taxi turned his head. He was looking out toward the source of light now, and against it he could see the dull shimmer of gold along the flank of Parade. Outside, toward the open air, there were other noises now. There was trampling through brush, and the sound of voices far off, answered nearer at hand.

Then two were speaking close by.

That was Pokey who cried out: "He's *got* to be around here, somewhere. Jim Silver and his horse can't evaporate, can they?"

"Don't ask me what the devil they can do," said Barry Christian.

"Well, I'll crawl back into this here cave," said Pokey.

"You fool," said Christian. "Even if a man could get back in there under the rock, how could a horse do it? Lie on its side and crawl like a snake?"

"Yeah," said Pokey. "But a man could get back in there."

"You'll find Silver where you find the horse," said Christian firmly. "I know it in my bones. I've always known it. There'll be no end to Silver until there's an end to the horse. The two of them are tied together."

"There's Babe yelling down there in the hollow. Blast him, he's the one that lost Taxi for us!" cried the high, snarling voice of Pokey.

"Babe did everything he was able to do," said Christian, with surprising moderation. "I was the fool to leave Taxi in the hands of Babe after I knew that Silver had started on the trail. There was no way for Silver to trail us, but I might have known that he would find us, in the end. And how could Babe tell that Scotty had been caught and gagged by Silver? There's no one to blame except the devil that's inside Jim Silver, and that devil I'll have out of his body. One day I'll see what his heart is made of, or he'll see mine."

He said this with a calm determination that baffled Taxi. It was as though the man had seen the future and knew to a degree what it held. And he thought of that intellectual and cruel face, and it seemed to Taxi that it would be worth while to die at once, if only he could first put a bullet through the brain, between the eyes of Barry Christian.

The voices retreated, after a time, and left Taxi to the long agony of his bruised body.

Half a dozen times, during the next few days, voices again came by them, very close, and half a dozen times they went away again before, at last, Silver said:

"We're going to chance it and get out in the sun. The sun may do more for you than I can."

There had been, in the interim, such care from the hands of Silver as it seemed only a physician could give. He went out once a day to go to a distance, cut a burden of grass, trap fresh meat, cook it, and then carry the supplies back to the darkness of the cave. That was how Taxi and Parade were supported during the interim of twilight in that refuge. Then, with his saddlebags as buckets, Silver carried in water for the horse and fell to his usual occupation of massaging the invalid.

He seemed to need no light; but, as one who knew every muscle like an anatomist, he carefully rubbed the battered body of Taxi. It was agony to endure. It was exhausting, at first, to such a degree that Taxi always fell into a long sleep, after the massage had ended. But with each treatment more use of his limbs returned to him.

He did not need to be carried, when Silver at last gave the word and they went from the inner into the outer cave. There, lying prone on the verge of the golden day, with the sun soaking through his clothes, reaching his body with healing fingers of warmth, Taxi saw the mystery solved.

The inner cave was blocked off from the outer by two great rocks, under which there was left a hole through which a man could barely crawl. But Silver, grasping the lower edge of one of those boulders, gradually managed to turn it until it fell clear and crashed against the side wall. Then it seemed to fit into an old notch, and Silver called to Parade, who came out like a huge dog, flat on his belly, crawling and scratching until he was through and at last stood in the sun and threw up his head to neigh his delight in the world.

"Stop him!" cried Taxi. "Don't let him whinny—they'll hear sure as shooting!"

Silver shook his head. "We've stopped playing safe. We're taking chances now," he said.

Taxi lay back and wondered at him.

In fact, Silver set to work to make a home of this place, since he had decided that they were to take chances and no longer live a secret existence.

He made a fireplace of stone, in front of the cave and just to the side of it, so that as little smoke as possible might blow inside. He cut down with a hand ax a quantity of pine boughs and saplings to build two huge, soft beds of the fragrant evergreens. He built two windbreaks that cost him a whole day's labor. And when the next storm came they had reason to be thankful for the shelter.

In the meantime, Taxi increased in strength each day. The diet was cold water, unsalted meat, and certain roots which Silver baked with the meats; besides, there were herbs to make a green salad and go down with the meat.

There was a great, hollow-topped rock near the entrance to the cave. That hollow Silver filled with water every day, and then built a fire about the rock until the water inside it was hot. To that he carried Taxi and gave him as warm a bath as he could stand, followed by massage.

That was a help, but most of all to make the cure, the heat of the sun was at work every day. Silver made Taxi lie out stripped in the white fire that fell through the trees, and the searching heat went to the very marrow of his bones.

Every day he could do more. He could crawl. He could prop himself up on his arms and sit with his back against a tree. Then he could pull himself up along the tree and stand. Finally he could walk, brief, tottering steps.

He was never still while he was awake. To regain control of himself was his present goal. He bent every energy of his keen brain to the task. As soon as he could use a muscle, he was at it constantly. He got a gun from Silver and, sitting under the tree, practiced for hours, making the draw from whatever part of his clothes held the weapon.

It was not like his automatics. It was a big single action Colt with a huge barrel that had, in length, at least four extra inches added. The trigger had been filed away. The sights were filed off, also. And the hammer worked on an easy spring, so that it could be fanned.

There was practically no conversation between him and Silver, because he felt it was dishonorable for him to ask Silver what the hidden purpose behind the rescue might be, and until Silver told him, there was a barrier between them. However, he could at least ask why this weapon pleased Silver more than an automatic.

Silver answered the question readily enough.

"When you use an automatic," he said, "the kick of the first shot throws the gun out of line for the second one. You're not placing every shot with care. You're sprinkling lead out of a hose, so to speak, and none of the drops may hit the bull's-eye. Besides, the mechanism of an automatic will go out of shape, now and then; and if it's only once in a thousand times, that once is enough to be the death of you, I suppose."

It seemed to Taxi a fine calculation of chances, this last bit of the argument.

As for the rest, he answered: "I'm fair with my automatics. They shoot pretty straight for me. Will you let me see you work?"

"Certainly," said Silver.

It had seemed to Taxi that there had been just a shade of boasting about the previous comparison between a single-shot, old-fashioned Colt and the newest pride of the gunsmiths. Now, moved by a malicious impulse, he picked up two small rocks from the ground beside him and tossed them high in the air.

"All right," said Taxi, and watched not the rocks but the effect on the man.

Even so, it seemed to him that there was no actual move of the hand to get a heavy gun from under the coat. There was merely a double flash and then the double report of a gun, fired from just a little above the hip.

Taxi looked up. But there were no longer two black spots falling through the air. The stones had disappeared.

Taxi continued to stare upward for a moment at the unstained blue of the sky. It was for him a moment of awe and wonder. In all his days he never had encountered a man who was his master with weapons, but now he realized that this big, brown-faced man was his superior as far as he himself was the master of some green novice, almost.

"Pretty good," said Taxi, and fell back into his usual long silence.

The day came, however, when he could endure it no longer. It was a bright morning. Down the slope between the trees he could see a solitaire, the loveliest of songsters, lifting itself from the top of a shrub by the wild joy of its own music and then descending again to its perch only to be blown upward again on an entrancing cloud of song. Something came out of that song into the soul of Taxi.

He could not exactly say what it was; but he knew that, as he listened, a great panorama unrolled in his mind. It was not of towering skyscrapers and shadowed streets and alleys that he thought, but he saw now big-shouldered and hard-flanked mountains, gaunt as athletes, thrusting their heads at the sky, the white of the summits hardly paler than the sun-drenched shining of the heavens. And it seemed to Taxi that he had found a thing which he could never live without again.

It was strange. It was like discovering a new food without which one could not exist and which could only be found far from one's old haunts.

The bird sang, and, as it ended, Silver said quietly:

"I've known people who shot singing birds."

That was all. Taxi could not tell why, but the words drove back a bolt in his heart and made him exclaim:

"Silver, why did you do it? Why did you risk your neck to help me? What can you get out of me?"

"Why did I do it?" asked Silver. He looked at Taxi with a strange twinkle in his eyes. "Why, I don't know," he concluded. He went on with his work of cutting up venison into gobbets of the right size to be impaled on a wooden spit and turned at the fire.

That was when Taxi made up his mind. Whatever went on inside the brain of Silver, the man was too cunning, too subtle for him. He would have to get away. He wanted with all his heart to ask Silver what plan they could execute together against Barry Christian. But he would ask no more questions. He decided, then and there, to escape from this too formidable companion the first time opportunity came his way.

CHAPTER XVIII

Departure

THE simplest and first idea was to leave in the night. The second thought, however, was better. At night, Silver slept more lightly than a wild cat, and, besides, the stallion gave his master warning whenever the least sound came near to the camp. It would be awkward to explain to Silver, if he were found stealing off in the middle of the dark. But every day Silver was gone for a considerable time, and that was when Taxi decided that he would make his start.

He had climbed the hill near the cave, and from the top of it he could look down across the valley where Parade had leaped the ravine. He could also see, across the higher level, two ranch houses. From one of those places he could "borrow" a horse and make tracks for the cabin where he had been a prisoner. The great Barry Christian probably was no longer there. He must have moved on long before. But perhaps there would be in the house some clew as to the direction in which the gang had fled.

So in the prime of the morning Taxi lay stretched on a bit of sunny turf and watched Silver saddle the stallion and prepare to ride off.

"You'll be able to stand a saddle before long," said Silver.

"Another week," Taxi answered.

"Another week?" echoed Silver, and then sighed a little.

It was the first time that he had shown the least impatience, and it seemed to Taxi that it was just the same as receiving marching orders.

The moment that Silver was gone, Taxi took a broad white chip and wrote on it with a scrap of charcoal:

DEAR SILVER: Sorry to go without saying good-by, but I'm getting overdue in other places. What your game was with me as one of the cards I don't know. Anyway, I owe you my neck and I'm a man who pays.

TAXI.

When he had written that, he reconsidered for a moment, remembering above all a certain smile that was often on the lips of Silver, a quiet and brooding smile which only came when he was in silence, looking across the sweep of the mountains, or contemplating Parade as the big horse grazed in the meadow. What went on in the head of Silver at those times baffled Taxi. It was the memory of these moments that made him doubt, to a slight degree, that he was right in attributing to Silver some practical motive in the saving of his life. However, this touch of conscience was by no means sharp. The whole experience of Taxi had been teaching him that one cannot get something for nothing in this world.

He stood up, put on his coat, and brushed it off, looking down at the cloth with a rueful face, for it was spotted with grease and bloodstains into which dust had worked deep. No cleaning process could ever make it presentable again.

Then he struck off across country at an easy run.

On the way, he decided that "borrowing" horses might be a bad idea. In this part of the world men were said to lynch horse thieves more readily than they strung up murderers. They made a fine point of the matter, saying that the greatness of the crime could not be judged by the value of the horse. There was a profound moral reason or superstition hidden somewhere in their minds.

So Taxi went straight up to the first ranch house, and when an old, bent man with a tuft of goat's beard on his chin came to the screen door, he said that he wanted to buy a horse.

The old man got out a pair of spectacles and put them on the end of his nose to stare at Taxi.

"What would a man be doin' out here in the middle of nowhere without a horse?" asked the rancher.

"I was heading for Horseshoe Flat," said Taxi, "and

last night, while I was asleep, somebody must have gum-shoed up and stolen my saddle. He got my horse, too, and left me to hoof it."

"Well," said the old man, "a gent that's ready to steal a hoss is ready to steal a saddle, too, I reckon. We'll go out and take a look at some ponies."

He took Taxi out to a big corral where stood a roan with an ugly Roman nose and a gray with a more dainty head.

"You take your pick," said the rancher. "We got one price on most of our mustangs. Either of them'll cost you fifty bucks, and I guess the gray's a likely lookin' pony, eh?"

"The gray looks well," said Taxi. "I'll take the roan."

The old man grinned suddenly at him. "You looked like a tenderfoot," he admitted. "But maybe they have hosses in your home parts, too."

It wasn't necessary for Taxi to tell him that human nature and human pastimes were very much the same in all parts of the world. Men in the East may ride differently, but some of them can ride and ride well. So he simply picked out an old saddle and bridle, paid his bill, and wondered, as he received his change, at the peculiarly slipshod methods of Barry Christian and his men, who had satisfied themselves by taking his guns and leaving him with all his money, to say nothing of the complete burglar kit which was tucked away in the seams of his clothes and in his shoes.

He rode straight across country, from that spot, and sent the tough little roan dodging among the pine trees that surrounded the house where Barry Christian had been, as confidently as though he had received definite notice that the gang had vacated the place.

Of course, he was right. There was not a sign of a human being about the cabin. When he went inside, he found many tokens of a quick departure. In the kitchen pantry there was still a good deal of flour in the bin, a quantity of canned goods on the shelves, and a fine ham totally untouched. He found an unopened can of tobacco in the living room, together with some books.

He went scenting through that house for something that might give him a clew to use on the road. He got down to the cellar, at last, where the morning sun slanted down the steps and made a thin slit of gold on the moist earth of the floor.

It seemed to him that he could see himself lying there, a ghost, with Babe sitting near by canted to one side in his chair, reading a newspaper by candlelight. The illusion was so strong that it chilled him and made him want to get out again into the full glare of the sun.

He paused, first, at the spot where the little buckskin sack of gold had been ranged. There on the ground glittered a few particles left from the handful which he had spilled on the night when he attempted his escape.

The sight of them made him feel again the old agony by which he had passed across the floor and up the steps.

Even the manner in which he had opened the locks of his manacles had not caused them to look for a picklock on his person. And in some ways, he decided, Barry Christian and his men were actually a simple lot.

He went back to the main floor of the house again, but still he could find nothing really worthy of his attention, except his own image as he went by a mirror. He stopped and stared at himself. He looked thinner and older. Here and there on his face appeared thin streaks of fading green—the last of the bruises which Babe had beaten into his flesh. And for the thousandth time he wondered, as he stood there, what he would do to Babe when fortune and his good right hand made him at last the master of the brute.

He remembered what "Tony the Greek" had done in that house on Eighth Street. Tony had walled his dearest enemy into the cellar foundations. Tony was a good mason, and he had built a neat new wall that was exactly like the other walls. He built in his enemy until the bricks and mortar came up to the chin of the man. Then he let him stay there, said report, for three days, until the poor devil went screaming crazy. Then Tony used to go down into his cellar and sit with a bottle of wine and sandwiches and eat and drink and laugh when the crazy man screamed, because it was a subbasement, and not a sound could drift up from it to the street. After a while, Tony built up the rest of the wall to the ceiling, over the yelling lips of the crazy man, and it was not for five years that the dead body was discovered when the house was torn down.

They never did anything to Tony for that neat bit of work. Tony had, in fact, gone up Salt Creek two years before the discovery was made.

And when Taxi looked back on that thought, he decided that Tony's way might be a very good way with Babe.

After Babe—or, really, before him—there was Charlie Larue. That would not be hard, and it would be very pleasant, because Charlie would never be able to face him again. Charlie's nerve was gone and would never come back so long as Taxi was in the vicinity.

Finally, there was Barry Christian.

That was a different matter. Even Jim Silver had not been able to put Christian in his pocket, except for one occasion. And, grudgingly, bitterly, Taxi surmised that Silver was a better man than he. Better, at least, with a gun, and armed with mysterious motives which were beyond human comprehension, motives that made him venture his life to rescue a stranger who had no possible claims upon him, motives that made him put himself inside the power of the Christian outfit for days and days to nurse the sick man.

Mere humanity could not account for this. There was something very deep about it, and Taxi felt a shuddering awe for a man whose secret purposes were so well and so darkly concealed.

He got out of the log cabin, at last, and remounted the roan.

Where should he go next? Somewhere Barry Christian and his men were probably splitting up the gold dust in shares and preparing to spend the profits. Somewhere Taxi must get on their trail again. But the West seemed very big to him, as he sat there on the horse, while the roan thrust out its stubborn head against the bit.

Something else was moving uneasily in the mind of Taxi. He could not place it, at first. It was like a hunger for a certain sort of food, just as a man will yearn suddenly for cheese and beer, or for steak and onions, and it was only after a long moment that he realized what the thing was that troubled him with desire.

He wanted to see the girl again!

That seemed to Taxi the strangest moment in his life, as he sat there among the pine trees with a triple man trail stretching dimly before him and realized that he wanted to see a mere girl. He tried to tell himself that she was simply a kitchen drudge. He tried to remember disagreeable things, such as the way her hair had been stuck in dark wisps against the perspiration of her forehead, and how the streak of dishwater had stained her apron, and how her hands had been reddened and roughened by hard work. But, though he could recall these things, he could also see in his mind how the youth and strength had kept rising and shining in her eyes. He could see the brown of her forearm and the round white of her upper arm. He could see the blue vein in it.

It was dangerous for him to go back to Horseshoe Flat. It was the last place in the world for him to go to, because when he was seen, he would be spotted, and word would go to Pudge, and from Pudge it would go to the gang.

Suppose that he brought an action against Pudge for assault and battery? He smiled at that. It would be a funny thing if he ever used the law on his side of the fence. It was too funny even to be thought of.

Suddenly he loosed the reins and started the roan straight down through the hills in the direction of the Flat.

CHAPTER XIX

Taxi Talks

THERE was time to waste, after he was close to the town. He spent it idly in a thicket, lying out on his stomach with his elbows on the ground and his chin in his hands.

He kept thinking. It wasn't about the Christian gang that he thought so much, but chiefly about Silver, and then about the girl. After a time, as the sun went down, he was not thinking of Silver at all, but only about the girl.

"I've been the fall guy, around here. I've been a dud. Every time she thinks about me, she laughs," he told himself.

Then it was dark, and he rode slowly in toward Horseshoe Flat. She would have finished serving supper, by this time. She would be clearing off the dishes from the long table. The men would be sitting about, rocking back in their chairs and smoking cigarettes. Some of them would use toothpicks of wood or quills. These fellows out in the West had queer manners. But small things don't matter in a man's make-up.

He got down to the town, rode around to the boarding house, tied the roan across the street, three houses up, and then came to the back door of the Creighton place. He had worked everything out, and now there was the rattling of dishes in the kitchen. She began to sing.

That darkened the mind of Taxi. As if she gave a rap about him! But of course she didn't give a rap. He was just a bum, a fall guy that every one kicked around.

It was a funny thing that he should have got her on his mind. Back there in the Big Noise there were some blondes who would have chucked everything to belong to him. There were some real steppers, who knew about him and how he could fade through steel walls and get right at the secret mind of the biggest sort of safes. They were ready to gamble on him. There was one that was almost perfect. She was a lady, practically. When she made up, you hardly knew that she had put on anything. Her cheeks were just natural—except that they were always the same. When she smoked, no red came off on her cigarettes. She had brains, that girl had. And she was all for Taxi.

"Taxi, when you're feeling restless," she had said, "come around and take *me* for a ride, will you?"

He had never gone to take her for a ride. She was just lost in a crowd, so far as he was concerned. He knew that when a man falls for a girl, he always gets into trouble about it. Some of the toughest mugs in the world have tumbled for a blonde and then talked too much. You can't help talking to a woman, it seems. You tell yourself that you won't, but just the same you talk, and after a while the blonde sells you out. That's the way it always goes. The prettier they are, the deeper they nick you.

And here he was, like a fool, in spite of all he knew, standing on the kitchen steps and preparing to go inside to talk to a kitchen mechanic. Well, he wouldn't be such a fool. He'd leave that place and never come back. But still he kept standing there.

The door jerked open. The song rang loudly in his ears. There was the girl standing above him. She did not start at the sight of a man standing there on the steps. She shaded her eyes with one hand and peered down at him, saying:

"Hello! Come to collect something, partner?"

Then she gasped. She caught him by the lapels of the coat and fairly dragged him into the kitchen.

There she held him, while her frightened eyes ran over him for a moment. Then she darted away and locked both the doors, pulled down the window shade, and leaned back against the drainboard by the sink, panting. She had finished the dishes. There were just some pans on the drainboard. The aluminum was covered with little bright scratches from the sand soap she had been using on it.

She still seemed frightened; she was still panting.

"My Jiminy, Taxi!" she breathed. "Am I glad to see you? Ask me, am I glad to see you!"

He couldn't ask her that. He made a cigarette and went over and stood by the stove. She watched him, and then broke out:

"Talk to me, Taxi! Tell me something! What's happened to you?"

"Well," said Taxi, "I've got my clothes all covered with spots. A lot of dust has happened to me."

He smiled at her, but she made a gesture as though she wanted to wipe that smile out.

"What happened in the saloon? Was Jim Silver right? Did Pudge lay you out? Who did the shooting? Where did the gang take you? What did Larue do? Who else was there? Have you seen Jim Silver? *What* has been happening?"

"I've been out in the open air getting a sunburn," said Taxi.

She folded her arms at that, and began to nod in a severely judicial manner.

Then she walked up close to him and stood there, examining his face with her eyes.

"Somebody's been beating your face off," she said. "I know what an old bruise looks like."

"Do you?" said Taxi.

"There's a big patch on the side of your head where the hair has hardly grown out at all. Is that where Pudge whanged you?"

He ran the delicate tips of his fingers over the place where Pudge had fitted his skull to the butt of the gun. He said nothing.

"Go on! Talk!" she urged.

"I've been having a rest cure," said Taxi. "I've been lying out in the sun and having a rest cure."

"Don't be such a great big man," she commanded. "Break loose and tell me something. You don't have to be such a great big man when you're around me. The harder they are, the quicker they break. You look as though you'd been broken all to pieces, Taxi."

He considered.

"No, I haven't been broken all to pieces," he said.

"You won't talk, eh?" she demanded, backing up from him a little.

A queer alarm ran through him.

"Are you angry, Sally?" he asked her.

"Not very," she said. "You have to act like a mug, I suppose. That's the way you see yourself and you have to act that way. But why don't you cut loose? There's no rope on you. Say something. Say you're glad to be back here in Sally's kitchen. Say anything."

"I wanted to say that," he answered.

"You wanted to say what?"

"Well, that I'm glad—"

He hesitated. He felt that he was making a fool of himself, and he flushed.

"Well, I'll breeze along," said Taxi.

After he had said that, he had to start for the door. He didn't want to go to the door, but what he had said compelled him. She got hold of his arm and pulled him around to face the light. Her violence startled him.

"You didn't come down here just to breeze along again in two seconds. *Why* did you come?" she demanded.

"I wanted to see you," said Taxi, compelled to truth because he could think of nothing else to say.

"Are you being bright and smart?" she asked, half of herself. "No; he means it, partly. He's only part Indian, and the rest of him is almost human, tonight. What part of you is Indian, Taxi?"

"Indian?" he exclaimed.

He touched the black gloss of his hair, more startled than ever.

"I have no Indian blood," he said.

She began to laugh.

"Why, you're only about four years old," she told him. "No Indian, eh? No, because even an Indian does a little boasting *after* he's come in from the warpath. Stop being dark and secret. I'll tell you, it does my heart good to see you again!"

"Does it?" said Taxi. "Do you mean that?"

"Do I sound as if I'm just making conversation?" asked the girl.

"I'm glad of that," said Taxi.

He looked up so that the black lashes no longer were a veil, and his pale, bright eyes burned against her own.

"It hit me all at once, up there in the hills to-day," he said. "I was hungry for something. I found out that I was hungry to see you again. So I came down."

She folded her arms again, and from that support raised one hand to her chin. Her head bowed. She studied him with an upward glance.

"What's this all about, Taxi?" she asked.

He said hastily: "I don't know. Nothing. I don't mean 'nothing.' It's about you, I suppose. Isn't it all right?"

"It's not just a line," she said aloud, but to herself. "He means it. Well, Taxi, you can go right ahead and talk like this as much as you want to. I like it. I like it a lot."

"I don't know what to say," said Taxi.

"Oh, no?" she asked.

"No," said Taxi. "I feel like a fool. I don't know what to say."

"If you can't talk, what do you want to do?" said the girl.

He considered. Then he answered: "I'd like to sit down there by the stove and watch you?"

"Would you?" said the girl. "Not wanting to step up and help me finish with the kitchen, are you?"

"No," said he seriously. "I'd rather sit still and watch you. I've been remembering your face quite clearly, but not clearly enough. I was wrong about the mouth."

"Were you?" said the girl.

"Yes. I thought it was too big."

"It is," she answered.

"I don't think so," said he. "It looks about right to me. All of you looks about right to me."

"What are you trying to do, Taxi? Make love to me?"

"Making love to you?" he exclaimed. "Love? Why, no. Look here, Sally. I wouldn't be that sort of a dog. You don't think that I'd be that sort of a dog, do you?"

He grew pale with anxiety. He came a little closer to her and, in the midst of making a gesture, found that he had taken hold of her hand. He said:

"I know what I am, and I suppose you guess what I am. I wouldn't be such a dog—to make love to a girl that's right. You don't think I'm that sort of a hound, do you, Sally?"

She kept peering at him earnestly, as though she were almost discovering something in the bright pallor of his eyes.

"I don't know what you are," said the girl. "Tell me what you are, Taxi, will you?"

"You haven't guessed? I'm a yegg, Sally. Safe cracking is my business."

"That ought to be a lot of fun," said Sally.

"Whatever you do, I hope you won't laugh at me," said Taxi sadly.

"I'm a mile and a half from laughing," said the girl. "There's a whole mountain between me and a laugh."

And straightway she was laughing. She stopped herself and studied his worried face for a moment.

"It doesn't make you sick to think of a yegg being in your house?" asked Taxi.

"I sort of like it," said the girl. "What else are you?"

"A jailbird," said Taxi.

"That goes with safe cracking. It always does," she

said. "It's about three weeks of safe cracking and three years in jail, isn't it, Taxi?"

He was silent. After all, she was not very far wrong. Something about her way of putting it made out Taxi and all other criminals mere fools, mere weak wits.

"Jail always for safe cracking?" she asked.

"No. They haven't caught me so often like that. But they try to run me up Salt Creek all the time. The cops want to frame me and run me up Salt Creek. That's why I've been in prison a lot. I beat the rap—but not entirely. I get a year or two out of it, for some reason or other."

"What's Salt Creek?"

"The electric chair."

"Ah?" said the girl.

He could see that that had struck her in the face.

"I'm saying the wrong things," said Taxi. "I don't know how to talk to women. I won't talk any more."

"You're saying the right things," she told him. "How do they try to frame you?"

"They always call it murder," said Taxi. "It's murder every time, according to the cops."

"What's murder?"

"They're down on me," said Taxi, "so they try to call it murder every time I drop a man."

She took a breath. She seemed to need it.

"I'm a fool," said Taxi. "I shouldn't talk like this. I won't talk any more."

"Go on, go on!" she whispered. "I want to hear every word. Taxi, when you say—when you speak about dropping a man, you mean shooting—you mean killing a man?"

"You know," said Taxi. "When somebody double-crosses you. Then you go for him, of course."

"Of course," whispered the girl faintly.

"He knows you're after him. That's what makes the game."

"Game?" murmured the girl.

"You see, if he knows that you're coming, then he'll get his pals around him. He won't sleep. He'll be in hell, and he'll be ready night and day. You just let him hang on the tree and get ripe. After a while you go and pick him off."

He laughed a little. His eyes went brightly into the past, remembering certain occasions.

She seemed to be cold. Even her voice trembled. Her eyes gave over narrowing and sharpening to pierce his mind and kept getting bigger and bigger.

"And then," said Taxi, explaining, "after that happens a few times, you have some enemies. They'll always be gunning for you. Sometimes they think they have you. It means a fight. Besides, there are always some of the big fellows who try to arm in on a successful business like mine. If you don't give them a percentage, they start a pack of gunmen after you. When that happens, I try to dodge the gunmen and get at the big fellows. That's the best part of the game, when you get at the big fellows. But there's always trouble. If you get a big fellow, you do time. That's all there is to it. You do time."

She began to shake her head.

"You're simply different, Taxi," she said. "I've never met anybody like you. I want to ask you another thing. Jim Silver left Horseshoe Flat to find you. Did you see him?"

"I'm like the rest," said Taxi mournfully. "They all told me the same thing. They all said that when I fell for a girl, I'd talk my head off."

She waited as though she knew he would say more. Then he said, very tersely:

"Larue and three more of 'em got me in the Round-up Bar. They took me out to a place where Barry Christian was living in the mountains. He set a mug called Babe to work beating me up to make me confess that I was working with Silver and tell Christian what Silver's plans were. Babe beat me to sleep, a couple of times. Then I found myself folded over the back of a horse. Silver was carrying me high, wide, and handsome, as you people say. Christian and some of his crew were chasing us. Even Parade couldn't carry double and beat that lot.

"Silver threw a dead tree trunk across a ravine, handed himself across it, and then called to Parade. He'd lashed me to the horse. Parade jumped the gap; and Silver hid me in a cave until the Christian outfit stopped searching for us. He took care of me till I could walk. I don't know what he had in the back of his brain. I don't know what he wanted to use me for. I asked him. He wouldn't say. So when I was able, I slipped away from him, got a horse, and then came straight back here. That's the biggest part of the story."

"Taxi," she cried, "what *would* Jim Silver have in the back of his mind except the wishing to help you?"

"Charity?" asked Taxi coldly. Then he shook his head and added: "Not in this world. When there were elves and fairies, maybe. But people don't throw away something for nothing in this day. Silver had something in the back of his mind. I don't know what."

"Jim Silver," said the girl, "is the finest man in the world!"

"Maybe," said Taxi. "But not that fine. He—"

The dining room door sagged softly open. The form of a man appeared there, vaguely seen, but there was plenty of light shining on the big automatic with which he covered Taxi.

CHAPTER XX

Captured

EYES less sharp than those of Taxi would have seen the gun, also. But he made out even the face in the shadow and recognized "Plug" Kennedy, who for seven years had dogged him since the days when Taxi was a precocious boy of the underworld. Whatever chances were to be taken, there could be none risked on Plug's shooting abilities. He was famous with a gun. He was almost too famous to be on the side of the law.

The voice of Plug drawled out the familiar word: "All right. Hoist them, Taxi!"

The girl whirled about. She leaped straight between Taxi and the leveled gun, crying:

"Run, Taxi!"

He hit her out of the path of danger with a back stroke

of his arm. She staggered off and crashed against the kitchen wall as Taxi lifted his hands till they were level with his ears.

"You fool!" said Taxi to her. "He'd shoot through ten like you to get at me."

"Fast work, Taxi," said the hard, slow voice of Plug Kennedy as he edged through the doorway and farther into the light. "One split part of a second more and she would have got something that was on its way for you."

She stood by the wall, the breath knocked out of her, gasping. Taxi wanted to gasp, also.

Plug Kennedy was drawing closer. He took short steps as though he were carrying a glass of whiskey filled to the brim. That was because he did not want to upset the silken fineness of his aim by jarring the gun out of line to the least degree.

"All right," said Plug. "Turn around, kid."

Taxi turned. He knew the technique and he turned slowly.

"Want 'em behind me?" he asked.

"Never mind," said Plug. "I've got a new idea for you. Just keep them up high. Touch the ceiling, Taxi."

Taxi stretched his arms. Plug, with a painful accuracy, laid the muzzle of his gun against Taxi's backbone. Then he reached in front and with his left hand fanned Taxi for weapons.

"Hey! No gun?" he demanded.

"I've been a little hurried lately," said Taxi.

"You're getting careless, kid," answered Plug. "I know people back in the Big Noise that won't believe me when I tell 'em that I found Taxi when he wasn't heeled. Looks like you're tryin' to make it easy for me, son!"

His left hand kept on fumbling. He drove the muzzle of the automatic harder directly against Taxi's spine.

"You got the old outfit in your clothes, the same as ever, eh?" said he.

"There's no better place for it, Plug," said Taxi.

"No," said Plug. "There's no better place, I guess."

He stepped back, all his movements soft and easy. Sweat of a mortal anxiety, no matter what his advantages of position were, was running down his face. He was like a man in a cage, handling a tiger.

"Now turn around," he said huskily. He took a pair of handcuffs out of a coat pocket.

Taxi, turning, slowly lowered his arms and held them out. The bright steel bracelets instantly clicked into place. The girl did not move, but she moaned aloud. He turned his head and looked at her.

"That's only a start," said Plug. "I know how fast you can shed anything in the way of a steel fit, Taxi. I've got something better than that for you, old son."

He drew out a pair of leather cuffs with a strong steel chain joining them. Clumsily, with one hand, he got one of the cuffs over the left wrist of Taxi and drew it tight with a buckle. The other cuff he used in the same way. There were four small, strong buckles on each of these leather cuffs, and he pulled each one tight.

When he had done that, he seemed to feel more at ease and unlocked the steel cuff that was on Taxi's left arm and snapped it over his own left wrist.

He began to sigh and smile.

"There!" said Plug. "Look over that system, Taxi. I thought it all out by myself. I worked the whole gag out by myself, old son, and it's a beauty, eh? You can shed the steel bracelets as fast as they're chucked on you, but nobody in the world can ever get these cuffs off without working the buckles. And look! The buckles are stiff, and the leather strap runs through three guards. Any child in the world could unbuckle those straps, but not without pulling and hauling. I keep that leather resined so that it sticks, almost like glue. And there you are, Taxi. You'll never get those off without high-signing me, eh?"

"It looks that way," said Taxi.

"You're bright, Taxi, but you won't think your way out of those cuffs all the way to the Big Noise, and I'm telling you."

"Perhaps not," said Taxi.

"Perhaps not is right," said the detective. "We'll barge along. Excuse me, lady. I'm sorry, but business is business, in these hard times."

She had not moved. It seemed to Taxi that she was incapable of movement. He turned with Plug Kennedy and went toward the rear door of the kitchen.

"This is the quickest way out," said Kennedy.

Then the girl came with a sudden rush.

"Hey, quit it! Back up!" commanded Kennedy.

She paid no attention. She had Taxi by the sleeves of his coat.

"I know that I'll never see you again," she told him.

Something came over him. He looked beyond her with his pale, bright eyes and said: "There's no steel can hold me. They don't build walls thick enough or high enough. I'm coming back to you."

He leaned over a little.

She made it easy for him, holding up her face, but he felt shy and awkward. His lips were trembling; he was trembling all over when he kissed her.

He was almost glad when he was outside of the room, at last, under the open sky, though he knew that he was on his way to prison. They went around to the front of the house, down the street, through an alley, and by a winding route came at last to a back door, through a cluttered back yard.

There Plug knocked three times, and the door was presently opened by none other than Pudge, the bartender.

CHAPTER XXI

Bound East

WHEN Pudge recognized his visitors, he jerked the door wide open. He invited them into a little back room and started rubbing his hands with pleasure.

"You got him, Kennedy!" he said. "I told you that you and me would be able to do business together. You can see it in our names. Plug and Pudge. That sounds like a team. And I told you my tip would be right. I knew he'd come back there. When the tough mugs get an idea about a girl, they're weak. They're so weak that they're soggy."

"They are," said Plug. "What beats me is that there was any girl at all. That's why I thought you were batty.

There's never been no girl before. But there's where old Father Time gets in. He softens up the hard ones. This girl is a peach, Pudge. Didn't she jump between him and my gun so's he could run or fight! And didn't he knock her out of the way instead of pulling a gun or a knife, or something! It's funny. He ain't the same as he used to be. He's all softened up."

Plug talked so slowly that it took him some time to make this speech.

Taxi said: "Plug, I don't ask favors."

"No, you don't," admitted Plug. "What's up?"

"Shut your mouth about the girl, will you?"

Plug Kennedy laughed. "All right," he said. "I'll shut up about her."

He kept on laughing. "He's all softened up," he said to Pudge again.

Pudge came close to Taxi. From his superior height he looked down on him carefully.

"Young feller," he said, "I'm glad to get you out of this neck of the woods. I see Babe's thumb marks on you; and you've got a memorandum from Pudge on your skull, out of sight. But I been thinking that before the wind-up, maybe you'd leave some marks on the two of us, and that those marks would never rub off!"

He turned to Kennedy.

"We can settle now," he said.

"I got it here," answered Plug.

He took out a wallet, opened it, and passed over a sheaf of bills inside a brown wrapper.

"That's exactly it," said Kennedy. "But you count it."

Pudge made a magnificent gesture.

"I ain't going to count it," he said. "If you held out something, you're welcome to it. It's a present, brother. That's how glad I am to see you taking this bundle of meat out of Horseshoe Flat."

He turned back to Taxi.

"Silver's going to be in the soup before long, kid," he said. "When we spotted your sign around Barry's old shack, we knew that you'd hit for Horseshoe Flat, and we knew that Silver would be hopping along the line you'd traveled. Maybe they've got him already, because the whole gang is sure to be back on the job at the old hangout by this time. There was more of the stuff that you know about. There was more of it to rake in; so they're back on the job, and they'll take in Silver for the extra profit."

He began to laugh, and rub his big, wrinkled hands together. So he followed them to the door and stood holding it open after they had gone out into the night.

"The train starts in fifteen minutes," said Pudge. "Don't be late for it. If you try to hold that hombre over in this town for one night, no one knows what'll happen. Hang onto him, Plug. Hang on hard. We don't want him back here!"

The door closed. They walked rapidly by dark alleys toward the railroad station, and Taxi found himself standing under the flare of the big gasoline lamp on the station platform while a crowd of idle hangers-on who were waiting for the Overland to come through, stood close up, staring at the handcuffs that proclaimed his status.

He kept looking down at the ground, according to his custom, merely noting their faces through the dark fringe of his lashes.

Then the Overland came, roaring. It seemed to Taxi that his heart speeded up as fast as the whirling of the wheels. This was almost his last moment of hope. There was still man power about him to sweep him out of the hands of Kennedy, if there were only something to set that man power in motion. But nothing happened. The wheels groaned against the brakes and the sanded tracks. The train shuddered to a stop, and Plug hurried Taxi up into a big Pullman.

Some passengers on the platform gave back with horror in their eyes when they saw the handcuffs. A whisper started that seemed to run the length of the entire train. And then the porter, with popping eyes, was showing them into their compartment.

Once in it, Plug Kennedy relaxed utterly.

As he flung himself down on the stiff cushions and bristling plush of the seat, he said to Taxi beside him:

"What puts you on edge, Taxi? Might as well relax, son. All the way across, I'm the one that has the hard luck. I can't close my eyes more'n half a minute at a time. I have the rotten luck on the trip. I cash in at the end of it, and you go to jail. But what the hell? You been here before! It'll be kind of restful for you, I'd think. A bird like you out in the big open spaces—why, it's bad for your nerves, I'd think!"

"Would you, Plug?" asked Taxi.

He smiled a little. Kennedy was silent, staring at him. The square face of Plug Kennedy was built like that of a bulldog, for receiving hard shocks with the least surface damage. It was hard for much emotion to register in that face, but a sort of brooding content that was almost like affection appeared in his eyes as he examined Taxi.

"So it's over, Taxi, eh?" he said. "A long rest for old Taxi now. When I take and look at you, kid, it does seem funny—what I mean is, the reputation that you've grabbed for yourself while you're still a pup! That's what eats me. That's what flabbergasts me!"

The train was still laboring up a long grade. Now it went over the top with a sudden quickening, a lessening of wheel noises and an increased roar of their running.

"What's the charge?" asked Taxi.

"Aw, what d'you care, Taxi?" asked Kennedy.

"Not much. I'm curious, is all. Who framed me?"

"Doheney. You might as well know."

"Old Rip Doheney, eh?"

"That's the boy that did it."

"It'll please Rip to see me behind the bars again. Or is he going to try to shove me up Salt Creek?"

"Not this journey. Just burglary, son. Just fourteen or fifteen years."

Plug laughed, as he finished.

Taxi, for a dreaming moment, forgot his own future as his mind reverted to another picture—Jim Silver returning to the house of Barry Christian on the trail of Taxi and finding the house a dark trap set for him. What was it that Silver had had in his mind? What was it that the girl had meant?

She had called Silver the finest man in the world. Well, she had been willing to throw her life away to help Taxi. She had proved that in the split part of a second back there in her own kitchen on this very night. It made Taxi dizzy when he remembered.

And suppose that Jim Silver were made of the same stuff?

Taxi ruled the thought out of his mind. There could only be one person in the world capable of doing something for nothing. And that one person happened to be a girl. He had found her. She was a dazzling brightness in his mind.

And yet, if only he were free to leave this train and fly back like a homing bird straight for the house among the hills—

He heard the voice of Plug Kennedy saying: "They've got some brains out here, sending the flash on to us as soon as they spotted you. They wanted you out of the way."

"They want me out of the way," admitted the soft voice of Taxi. "Rip Doheney, eh? What sort of a job does he want me for?"

"Big diamond robbery in Pittsburgh."

"I haven't been in Pittsburgh for three years."

"That's all right. The boys know that you're fond of the ice. And this was a big job done in a big way by one man working all alone. Exactly the sort of a job that you'd be likely to tackle, Taxi. Nice and clean and neat and no clews left. Nice and neat. That house was opened up like an oyster shell and cleaned out and closed up again. So they'll soak you for the job. Something had to be done about it. The people that lost the diamonds were big birds. They raised a holler. Doheney saw he couldn't get a clew, so he decided, when we heard you were out here, to try to get you and slam you for the job. It's business, Taxi."

"Yes. It's business," murmured Taxi.

"Too bad, in a way," said Plug Kennedy. "Maybe you can hitch out of it if you have enough hard cash to hire a good lawyer."

"No," said Taxi. "My record's too long. No use wasting money on a lawyer, because they're sure to soak me anyway, in the long run. They're used to slamming me, so they'll slam me again. And Rip Doheney knows how to bring on the cooked-up testimony."

He fell into deeper thought than ever.

Then he said: "Tell Rip something for me, will you?

Tell him that when I'm out of this mess, I'm going to get him."

"Hey!" cried Plug. "What's the idea? What's the new, big idea? You never go gunning for the cops, Taxi. You use your ammunition on the other yeggs. You know that!"

"The trouble is," said Taxi, "that now my time means a lot to me."

There was a long pause in the talk, after this.

"I've talked too much," said the detective finally.

He was gloomy about it. He kept shaking his head.

"Rip would have showed up in the case, anyway," said Taxi, in the tone of one giving comfort. "You don't need to blame yourself too much."

"That's true," agreed Plug. "He would 'a' showed up. But you're different, Taxi. You used to take it on the chin without batting an eye, but now you're all worked up."

"I'm seeing things," said Taxi. "I'm seeing that you private detectives are as bad as the yeggs, most of you. Watch me carefully, Plug, because if I manage to find a way out of these cuffs, I'm going to open you up before I leave the train."

Plug leaned forward and stared at him.

"You *are* changed," he muttered. "You're ready for Salt Creek, at last! If I had my way, I'd railroad you up the Creek on this here job!"

"Thanks," said Taxi, and lifting the dark shadow of his lashes, he smiled at his companion with the full brightness of his pale eyes.

Afterward, he sat back against the seat and fell into profound thought. If there were a possible way of doing it, he had determined in the course of these few minutes that he would break away from Plug if it cost him his life to do so. Back yonder among the hills, only the devil himself could tell what danger Jim Silver was approaching.

Even the Barry Christian outfit, even Pudge, seemed to feel confident that there was nothing Silver would not dare for the sake of a friend. But would Silver risk his neck for the sake of a man who had deserted him and ran away? The thing seemed impossible, but a vast, hungry curiosity ate up the soul of Taxi.

There was something new out here in the air of the

West. The breathing of it was different. The taste of the ozone was cleaner and went deeper in the lungs. There was more for the eye to grasp inside the circle of a vaster horizon, and perhaps it was also true that the souls of men were cut to larger dimensions?

"Fairly tales! Bunk!" said Taxi aloud.

"Yeah? What?" asked his companion.

Taxi said nothing. He kicked his toe into the plush of the opposite seat and looked at the dust mark that was raised from the plush.

"And I'm going to take you at your word, Taxi," said Plug Kennedy. "Mind you, I'm going to take you at your word and the first time I even *think* you're raisin' your hand, I'm going to drill you, kid."

"Better take the burglar kit off me," said Taxi. "Better take it out of my clothes. I can do a lot with tools like the kind I have in my duds, Plug."

"Thanks," said Plug. "That good advice can go with you, too!"

"Hard words," said Taxi.

"Right here with my eyes open I sit," said Plug. "And if you can work something on me, kid, while my eyes are right on you, you're wonderful. I'll write a book about you!"

"You forget, Plug," said Taxi, "that if I get loose, the first thing I do will be to rub you out."

Kennedy stared at him.

"You've changed since you've gone and got yourself a girl," said Plug. "I'll tell you how you've changed. You talk too much."

Taxi laughed. He kept on laughing softly while he almost closed his eyes. The matter of his mirth seemed to endure.

He scratched his leg. From the outside seam of the trousers, he took out a small picklock between the second and third fingers of his left hand.

The train flashed by a small town, streaking out the lights into tiny comets.

"Scratch my right wrist where the handcuff is," said Taxi. "Those steel cuffs are always able to start me itching."

"Scratch your own wrist," advised Plug Kennedy, growing more ugly.

"All right," said Taxi.

"And mind you, I'm watching."

"Look close, Plug," said Taxi. "Because something's likely to happen to you at any minute."

"Yeah?" said Plug. He dropped his right hand into his coat pocket. "I've got a little iron lady here ready to talk to you, boy. I know you're kidding now. But I just want you to know that I'm *not* kidding."

"All right," said Taxi. "But keep your eyes open."

He put his left hand over on his right wrist and scratched carefully under the steel of the handcuff. That slow, wobbling movement enabled him to insert the pick-lock into the keyhole.

"You're getting like a dog—gotta scratch your skin, eh?" said Plug. "Why don't you—"

He broke off with a grunt of terrified surprise and jerked the gun out of his pocket, for his ear had heard a faint, metallic sound as the lock of the handcuff gave way and the steel snapped outward, worked by its spring.

Taxi jerked up both his manacled hands at the same moment and landed them under the chin of Plug.

It was a good punch with so much lift in it that it brought Kennedy to his feet.

There he wavered, the gun pointing straight at Taxi's breast.

The handcuffed youth stepped in, clubbed his two hands, and brought them chopping down on the chin of the detective. Plug Kennedy dropped the automatic on the carpet and slumped to the floor.

Taxi kicked the gun aside. Plug was quite right—the straps of those leather handcuffs were hard to work. But his fingers were steel springs, and in a moment he was free. Plug, in the meantime, had begun to groan and kick out. As his senses returned to him, he seemed to think that he was in the middle of a fight and grappled the legs of Taxi.

Butting the muzzle of the automatic against the temple of the detective, Taxi said: "It's all over, Plug."

Kennedy lifted his amazed face and stared.

"Something happened," said Plug. "I dunno what. But something happened, and—"

"Get up and sit down over there," said Taxi. "I picked that lock while I was scratching my wrist."

Kennedy rose from the floor and sat down. Taxi tossed the automatic on the other seat and leaned over the detective, proceeding to bind and gag him.

It was an open invitation for Kennedy to grapple with him, but Plug Kennedy was not such a fool. He knew too many stories of men bigger, stronger, better-trained than himself who had tried their bare hands on Taxi, and the stories all ended in just one way.

Kennedy sat still and allowed Taxi to tie him up.

"And I had my eyes open," said Kennedy. "That's what eats me. I had my eyes open!"

CHAPTER XXII

The Trail To Danger

WHEN the emergency signal stopped the Overland, it was a moment before the excited conductor got to the compartment of Plug Kennedy and entered, shouting:

"What fool sort of a joke—"

Then he saw Plug lying on the floor, where he had rolled from the seat in his frantic efforts to get to the door and make a noise, though the omniscient Taxi had assured him that struggles would get him nowhere. But Plug was a determined man. Now he lay on the floor with his eyes peering out over the swelling of an apple-red face.

When the conductor pulled out the gag, the voice of Plug issued in a siren screech:

"Get Taxi! He's on that other train! He's on that freight that just pulled past out of the station. He's on that and—get him, or he'll wreck half the Rocky Mountains before sunrise!"

But Taxi was already scooting back toward Horseshoe Flat as fast as a strong engine could take him and a lean train of empties. Yet it seemed slow progress to him, so that he was tempted, now and again, to get off the train and take to his feet. All his muscles twitched and strained as he crouched on the floor of a box car and saw, through the open door, the slow procession of the hill against the distant, bright, unheeding stars.

Over and over again he saw the great form of the golden stallion looming through the night among the trees that surrounded the house of Barry Christian among the mountains; he saw Jim Silver coming slowly out of darkness to explore the place. But not even the prescience of a Jim Silver could equip him with skill to read the dangers of an unlighted house where enemies might be lurking. He would need more than the eyes of a cat.

At last the train entered the long, swift down grade toward Horseshoe Flat. But still there remained the getting to the horse and then the ride through the hills. And after he arrived there, what could he do?

In fact, Jim Silver had gone on the trail of Taxi, though not without some misgivings. The sense of kind had not been in him when he was with the man from the underworld but rather an immense curiosity that drew him from moment to moment. It had seemed incredible that a man could have the qualities of Taxi, the courage, the nerve, the brain and heart of steel without at the same time possessing some of the gentler characteristics. But the man had seemed incapable of deep emotion. He was like an Indian—able to remember a grudge forever, to keep to a blood trail with unshakable determination, and to endure the worst torture with locked jaws and a vacant eye. He was like a tool with an edge of the finest temper, able to work in hardest steel and in fact never used for anything else.

What made Silver finally take up the way of the fugitive was, as a matter of course, not purely a regard for this man whom he could hardly call a friend but rather a point of pride that intrigued him and led him on; for Taxi had plainly inferred that there must be some secret motive and some hidden spring of action that induced Silver to undergo such danger for him. It would be an ironic satisfaction to do Taxi one more good turn and then bid him good-by.

That Taxi would be in need of further aid, Silver had not the slightest doubt, because he knew enough of the nature of the man to understand that he would never rest content until he had repaid the torments which he had endured at the hands of Christian's men. Taxi would certainly go on the back trail to get at them, and if he did, he could hardly humanly hope to handle such a crew. His skill might be great but so was theirs. Besides this, he knew the genius of Barry Christian which was able to work in the dark of other men's intentions.

So Silver, after much time spent in brooding, finally took up the trail.

It was a hard task. He was busy until dusk getting the dim footmarks off the ground until he was able to strike out the line which Taxi had followed in coming to the farmhouse. The old man of the ranch told him freely enough about the manner in which Taxi had picked out the roan horse.

"You can't tell a man's brains by the clothes he's wearin'," said the veteran. And he pointed out how Taxi had ridden away, and indicated the gap among the hills through which he had disappeared.

"The sort of a gent," said the old man, "that you'd expect to see turnin' up again, somewheres—in a book, or his picture in the newspaper, maybe."

Jim Silver could agree with that.

When he came through the gap in the hills and made sure that the line Taxi was riding led almost straight back toward the house of Barry Christian, he shook his head and brought Parade to a halt.

To bait the lion was one thing, but to run straight into the lion's mouth was quite another, and to go back near that house would be to put one's head in the lion's mouth with a vengeance. In Silver's mental picture of the world, his spot was preëminently marked "Danger."

Then he let Parade drift ahead. He swore through his set teeth. He told himself that to have beaten Barry Christian once on such a spot of home ground was enough. To try it twice was suicide. But as he reached these very reasonable conclusions, he could not help remembering other things, such as the faint, dubious smile that used to appear in the face of Taxi, and the pale, almost inhuman brightness of his eyes when they looked up with a question, perhaps once a day.

So he kept to the trail. For he felt that whatever Taxi was, he was a most remarkable human machine. What that machine could accomplish he was unable to tell, but he guessed at great things.

Women have an instinct about men unless they are outright blind with love. And Sally Creighton, a most level-headed young lady, thought a good deal of Taxi. So Silver decided that he would trust to his own cold judgment and to Sally Creighton's instinct and therefore call Taxi a risk worth taking.

It was well after dark before he got to the vicinity of the Christian place. And it was long after that before he had worked his way with infinite caution through the night and come close to the house.

When he left the back of Parade, he felt as though he were leaving a secure ship at sea and committing himself to stormy waters. He went around the cabin first, with a soundless step, keeping very close to the wall, listening, listening, destroying all other faculties so that his sense of hearing could be more acute.

He heard nothing.

There was no moon, as yet, but the sky was speckled with the brightness of the stars that showed their faces as they only will to mountain dwellers. Against those stars he saw the trees go up, the pines making black, jagged points, like the heads of fish spears, barbed.

He saw nothing else. The air was cold. The world was frozen still. Not a wolf howled, not a coyote dared to bark in the distance. There was not even the still, small crackling sounds that, to the attentive ear, are usually heard around a house by day and night, from the warping timbers.

There was nothing present, he could safely say. But when he ventured on opening a door, he was by no means sure. For the slight draft that entered ahead of Silver sent long, ominous whispers down the space inside.

He forced himself to step into what he still felt might be a trap. And as he passed down the hall, he felt along the wall with his hand on this side, and then on that. He walked with steps more careful than those of an Indian. There was not a sound except that of his own breathing.

He found a door to the left.

When he opened it, he was sure, from the naked presence of the unseen chamber, that it was a big room. Something about the air told him that.

He stepped across the threshold and immediately to the right. Instinct made him do it, because when a man enters a place of danger, it is generally better to get away from the threshold and the straight line toward the door as soon as possible.

After he had managed to put a little distance between himself and the door, he again went forward in his original line.

He encountered a chair. With the soft touches of his hands, he circumnavigated it and went on. And all the while small worms of fear were crawling in his flesh and in his brain telling him of danger, danger, more terrible because so unseen. The cold poison of fear worked in his soul.

Then something hardly stronger than a spider's thread touched his breast.

He knew what it was with a swift and peculiar prescience. It was a thin silken thread stretched there for the very purpose of detecting the presence of a stealthy marauder like himself. He tried to leap back, catching at his gun at the same time. But a rope hissed in the air, a noose gripped him, pinning his arms to his sides, and the voice of Pokey went screeching, screaming through the darkness:

"Lights! I've got him! Lights!"

CHAPTER XXIII

Dynamite

THE strong pull on the rope jerked Silver off his feet. He tried to regain them, whirling over on his face, but now lights were unshuttered on either side of the room and streamed at him. In the path of them, men ran in at Silver, pinned him down, bound him with precise and rapid skill, hand and foot.

He was placed in a chair beside the cold hearth at the end of the room; he was tied strongly into that chair.

As his spinning brain steadied and settled, he could see all around him the men of the great Barry Christian. He saw Scotty's glistening black mustache, and the infantile brutality of Babe, and above all the whining, snarling devil, Pokey, who was in an ecstasy because of the success of the device that had been his suggestion.

It was nothing new—simply a cord with which Pokey was in touch, and a noosed rope suspended in the air with one end of it secured in Pokey's hand.

"When the door opened," yelled Pokey, "I knew that I had him. I knew it—I knew it! I laughed to myself. I've got him, I says to myself. Silver or Taxi, I've got him. And then—bingo! I noosed him. Can I fish in the dark? I ask any of you, can Pokey fish in the dark?"

He kept on laughing and exclaiming about his prowess, until Charlie Larue said:

"Aw, shut up, will you? You've talked enough."

"Let him talk," broke in the soothing voice of Barry Christian. "When a man of mine has turned a trick like that, I like to hear him talk. It does me good to hear him talk. Here, John, light the fire. Build it big and light it. It's the last fire that we'll ever warm ourselves in front of in this house, John."

The Chinaman came trotting, his braided queue jerking

up and down behind him, his pock-marked face grinning. His face, it seemed to Silver, was the physical index to the ugliness of all their souls. Nature had put no mask on him, and his reality was almost a relief.

The fire blazed very soon. Barry Christian pulled up a chair opposite that of Silver and lighted a cigarette. It was not a handmade smoke, but the finest Turkish that money could buy. And the great Christian drew every breath of it deeply into his lungs before he let it slowly perfume the air of the room.

The men stood by as at a moment of historical importance which each strove to record in his memory. They kept looking from the face of Silver to that of Christian, and back again. They were still. Their eyes were bright and unsmiling. Every gesture, every word, they drank in to the utmost.

"Babe, go out and walk the rounds of the house," said Christian.

"Me? Not me, chief!" exploded Babe.

Christian looked up with an eye of cold gray steel, but then he understood and merely laughed.

"All right, Babe," he said. "You've had some hard work to do in the cellar, not so long ago. Somebody else can take a turn at doing the dirty work."

He was about to tell off another man for the task of walking guard when a voice called far away through the night.

It was Charlie Larue who got to a window first and threw it open, while Christian stood over Silver with a gun loaded, ready to end him in case they were forced to run for it.

The voice in the night called again. And Larue shouted instantly:

"Come on, Pudge!"

He closed the window and turned with a broad grin.

"It's old Pudge," he said. "I know the roar that walrus has."

"Go let him in," said Christian, and Larue disappeared.

A brief silence followed, with Christian running his eyes slowly over the face of Silver, and Jim Silver calmly eyeing Christian. Their hatred had reached the point of perfection; it was calm.

Pudge came in. They could hear the rumbling heartiness of his voice from the distance, and the weight of his step. Then he entered, panting.

"I come up to give you boys some news," he said. "Taxi's gone."

Silver lifted his head a little. That news made the moment perfect. His whole adventure had been foolishly in vain and Taxi was dead before he had started, perhaps!

"Gone? You mean dead?" asked Charlie Larue anxiously.

Pudge turned his head to Larue and shrugged his fat shoulders.

"Better than dead," said Pudge. "He's on the way to jail. He's on the Overland, headed East. They're going to put him away for keeps. Maybe it'll be Salt Creek. Maybe it'll be twenty years. I dunno. They got him framed, and the beauty of it is that he didn't do the job he'll do time for!"

Pudge was so pleased by this picture of the future of Taxi, that he broke out into hearty laughter. The others were silent.

"Twenty years won't kill him," said Charlie Larue thoughtfully. "It'll only make him harder."

"Quit grouching, Charlie," said Pudge. "I know you don't like that hombre, and you got plenty reason, but—"

Here, for the first time, he saw through the men who had gathered about him the form of Silver, lashed into the chair.

"Holy smoke!" shouted Pudge. "It ain't Jim Silver? You mean to say that all our troubles are going to be finished on one day?"

"This trouble, Pudge," said Christian, "is going to vanish away!"

And he waved a graceful hand toward Silver.

Pudge came slowly forward. He dragged off his hat with a gesture that caused a long lock of his hair to tumble forward on his face.

"Silver," he said, "I've wished it. I've laid awake at nights and wished it. But I never hoped to see it. Honest, I never hoped to see you tied up like a pig for market! Barry, what's going to happen?"

"You can't guess, Pudge?" asked the gentle voice of Christian.

"Aw, sure. I can guess," said Pudge. "But what way?"

"That's it," said Christian. "We want to determine the way of Silver's exit. Because there ought to be a celebrated finish for a celebrated man. Am I wrong, boys? How about it?"

"You're right," they muttered.

"Start your minds working," said Barry Christian. "I want to talk to you a little about this man. All of you know a little about him, but none of you really know enough. Not really enough. Sit down, make your smokes, and give me some attention."

They obeyed these instructions. Pudge had a habit of wiping his hands even when they were not moist from his duties behind the bar. Now he sat very still, not smoking, but wiping his hands as he looked with awe and with content toward Jim Silver. The others made themselves comfortable.

"There was a time, boys," said Christian, "when the West was the West. By that I mean, there was a time when it was free. A fellow could follow his own fancy. There were a few sheriffs and deputies and federal marshals scattered about, but not enough of them to bother a man, really. It was a golden age, boys. A fellow could spread his elbows at the board—and when the board got a little too hot for his elbows, he could ride off into the hills and wait for things to cool down a little, and then he could return and try his luck again. Am I right?"

"You're right, chief," said Pudge, who being the oldest man took it on himself to answer.

"We were not bothered a great deal. It was a happy time. And then a man who wasn't a sheriff or a marshal, a man who had no business interfering, started on our trails."

Christian turned and looked at Silver. "He wanted trouble. He loved it. He ate trouble and he drank trouble. If he'd had the nerve of the rest of us, he would have gone against the law and taken his fun where he found it. But he didn't dare to do that. He was afraid. He was yellow, really, in his heart, because he was afraid of the law."

"Sure he was!" said Scotty, with a sudden acid anger.

Christian paused, controlling the passion that began to make his eyes burn. Then he continued:

"As a matter of fact, Silver wanted the pleasure of man hunting, and he didn't want the penalties. So he crawled over to the safe side of the fence. When he was on the side of the law, of course every time he managed to sneak a bullet into one of us, the people applauded. They cheered for him. I've seen in a newspaper, and a big newspaper that has a lot of authority and influences a lot of minds, the remark that one man like Jim Silver was worth more to the cause of law and order than any hundred sheriffs in the land. It's stuff like that, out of the papers, that makes Silver's life happy. That's what he lives for—newspaper gabble of that sort. And he's distinguished himself up and down the land by running us down. There's been no more mercy in him than there has been in a greyhound after rabbits."

He paused again, for again his emotion began to master him. But at last he was able to continue:

"I want you to remember that there was a time when I had a system that couldn't be beaten. I had you boys around me, and we lived a happy life. I had other men, too. There wasn't a one of them that I couldn't trust. And everything was done in secrecy, quietly, without a fuss. We did no real harm. We didn't settle down on one part of the range till we broke the back of it. We moved around here and there. We had friends among all the ranchers, all the little fellows with places scattered around through the hills.

"When they saw one of us, they took us in. They knew that we meant ready cash for our meals and everything that we took. They knew that when we came by in a pinch and needed a horse, it was worth while for them to trot out the best horses they had and give us a pick. The bill might not be paid till a month later, but it would be paid in hard cash then, and they could charge two times the real price of the horses. There were hundreds of men squatted around through the mountains, decent, honest fellows, who would have laid down their lives for us. Am I wrong?"

"I remember those days," said Scotty, with a sigh. "A man could live then. It was a gentleman's life. That's what it was. Then this hound came along and busted everything up!"

"And in those days," said Barry Christian, "there was nothing known. Not one man in twenty thousand knew what I looked like. There was just the name of Barry Christian that boys who were on the make knew was worth hitching to. And the people who worked with us didn't know me. It was simply a name, a sort of a trademark that told every one our work was going to be clean. Sheriffs hated the thought of us. Posses couldn't be raised to chase us, because they caught hell when they got close. And then everything changed. Everything!"

He turned back to Silver.

"Silver," he said, "when I look at you, I can hardly keep my hands off you!"

"Thanks," said Silver. "From my way of thinking, old son, that's a compliment."

Christian went on: "He chose to walk in on me, and life has been hell for all of us, ever since. The ranchers suspect us now. Too much has been published about us. And as for me, my face has been published all up and down the land—with a reward stacked on the top of my head, so that I hardly dare to trust the men of my own crowd!

"But now, boys, there is going to be a change. We've come to the end of the trail and after to-night we're going to be able to turn back to the old days. We're going to build ourselves the same reputation we had before. We're going to make sheriffs turn sick at the thought of us. We're going to find clients here and there in the mountains. A new deal for every one all around, and the past forgotten and bygones gone forever. Because to-night Jim Silver dies!"

It seemed to Silver, as he listened, that there was in reality a golden age of happiness and careless, secure adventure in the picture which the leader had painted. He could see the reflection of it in the bright eyes of the men before him.

"How?" asked Pudge. "That's what I wanta know. How?"

"This way!" said the squeaking voice of the Chinaman.

He came in carrying a heavy tarpaulin bundle in each hand.

"Hey, you fool, get out of here with that!" yelled Charlie Larue. "The Chink has the dynamite!" he explained.

No explanation was needed. The gang scattered in haste as John walked up to Silver and slid the two big bundles under his chair. Then he undid a long coil of fuse that had not been cut and snaked it out in a curving pattern upon the floor, until it was all distributed.

Then he said, with appropriate gestures: "You light here. Jim Silver watch the fire come. We wait outside. Poom! Jim Silver gone."

Christian went on: "And then the fire burns the house and sends the bits of Silver up in smoke—and there you are! He's a famous man, boys, and if he disappears, there'll be a search down to bed rock. But that won't bring them to smoke and ashes, I think! John, I always knew that you were something more than a cook and a smuggler. Now I know how much more!"

The full beauty of the idea seemed to be dawning on the others, little by little.

Babe bawled out: "And there Jim Silver sits like a king on a throne, and he sits and watches the fire come snakin' along the fuse at him. And he counts the seconds, and the time goes pretty fast and then—boom! That's the end of Silver."

He began to laugh, thundering his mirth through the place.

"Fix the fuse," said Christian. "John, you had the idea, and you can have the glory and the fun, too. Fix the fuse and light the far end of it."

The cook was instantly at work, singing a queer little tuneless song as he busied his hands.

Christian lingered near Silver.

"I hate to leave you, Jim," he said. "In a sense, this will be a rather empty world, with you out of it. It will be too simple. There will be no one to match my brain against. And yet I'll have to struggle along as well as I can. I wish I could be here till the last, Jim, and see you sitting on your throne, as Babe calls it, until you're taken at one step to hell. Jim, I almost feel like shaking hands. Good-by, Silver!"

Silver said nothing, but lifting his head, he looked calmly into the face of Barry Christian. And Christian, running his fingers through the long silk of his hair, stared down at his victim and smiled.

Then he turned on his heel.

"Scatter out of here, all of you," he said, seeing that the end of the fuse had been lighted and that the light of its burning was sputtering across the floor, making the snaky fuse line shudder and leap. "Get out and stand by to see the pieces of Jim Silver start skyward. Get out. I want to lock every door. There's only two or three minutes before that fire hits the dynamite."

CHAPTER XXIV

The Explosion

THERE was one auditor of the words of Christian who was not in the room. That was Taxi, who had flattened himself against one of the windows, so that he was able to see much and hear everything.

Now he dropped to the ground and raced to the rear of the house. The men were already swarming out the side door. The voice of the Chinaman came singing through the kitchen as Taxi dropped into a patch of brush just behind the kitchen door.

The Chinaman came out, locked the door behind him, dropped the key into his pocket for all the world as though he might have to use it again, tossed his queue over his shoulder, and went off at a dogtrot toward the little shed at the rear of the house.

It was the best place to secure complete shelter from any flying fragments from the explosion. Taxi already had glanced into it and seen there a single mule loaded with a small pack. There were no horses in the shed. The gang, of course, would have left their mounts in the distance.

Taxi, as he kneeled in the brush, kept swearing in a soft whisper. In a few moments Jim Silver would be ended, but the calm face of Silver as he had looked back at Barry Christian would never die out of Taxi's mind.

He had known, as he stared with aching eyes through the crack in the window, that this man was, in fact, capable of every good thing that he had dreamed of him, and incapable of the evil. The quiet with which he sat there, and the steady, firm eyes, somehow had told Taxi.

There was only firelight in that room now, and the sputtering, dancing end of the fuse as the fire ran up its coiling length toward the dynamite. But there would be enough light to show Jim Silver all his life. Perhaps among other things he would see the face of Taxi, a stranger, an unknown man, for whose sake Silver was to die!

Taxi stood up among the brush.

There was nothing to do. He could hear the heavy locks turning with a clank as big Barry Christian turned the key in door after door, to seal Jim Silver with his fate.

There was nothing to do. Except, afterwards, to run them down, one by one!

And then he saw himself leaning over the locks in that dark house, fumbling with the picklock, struggling forward, striving to get at the man who sat there waiting for death. He would be working like that when the explosion came and put an end to them both.

"Scatter out, boys," said the voice of Barry Christian, in the distance. "Scatter out and get under the trees, in case that explosion sheds something on us out of the sky. Watch yourselves, lads!"

What a cheerful ring in his voice—and Jim Silver in yonder, waiting for death, alone!

Like a ghost, Taxi was out of the brush and on his knees at the back door. There were no eyes to watch him. All the men of the gang were gathered far forward to enjoy the full flare and crash of the explosion. What was left of the house would soon be flaming from the embers of the fire that burned in the living room.

The kitchen lock opened, but with a slowness and a difficulty which augured ill for the other locks. This lock must be used more constantly than the others. The rest were apt to be more difficult because of rust.

Now, like the edge of a sharp knife, the flashing light in Taxi's fingers divided the darkness, right and left.

The next doorknob glinted. He was at the lock in an instant. And the little picklock trembled at the heavy inwards of the metal contrivance.

Two minutes or three minutes, Barry Christian had said, before the fire reached the dynamite.

The hands of Taxi shuddered. It seemed to have been longer than two or three minutes. It seemed twenty or thirty minutes. His heart was beating slowly. His heart was stopping. For time seemed to be rushing like a stream of lightning past Taxi.

He could do nothing with the lock. His mind was urging him to leap from the house, to run to a distance, to hurl himself face downward on the ground before the explosion blew him into eternity.

He jumped to his feet.

Then with the ice-cold hand of his will he took hold of himself, bowed his knees, made himself bend over the doorknob. His iron will would not even let him begin at once but forced him to count three slowly, deliberately, while the chill sweat trickled down his face.

After that, he had himself in hand.

He opened that lock with a mere gesture, as it were, though it seemed a slow gesture to one racing against time in that manner.

The flashlight touched the door on the farther side of the dining room. He was instantly at it. The lock was stiff. It was soldered firmly with rust. He threw away the small picklock and took a larger one. It would not fit the wards!

He had to turn and find the bit of steel he had just discarded. Calmly, slowly he played the ray of light across the floor, since haste would be sure to miss it. He found it, reached it with a tigerish bound, returned to his work —and in an instant that door was open.

He was in the hall. The living-room door was there in front of him. He went at it savagely, yet delicately. He found the heart of it. The bolt moved among the wards. The door yielded itself to his hand, and snatching the door open, he looked in and saw the running fire of the fuse right at the dynamite.

He shrank, then hurled himself forward. His hands and arms seemed to have the courage and not the rest of his unwilling body. His hands gripped the sides of the doorway, and his arms threw him forward, stumbling, until as he drew nearer, he saw that the fire in the fuse had not actually covered the last two feet of the cord.

He put his heel on the fuse and ground the fire out. Then he began slashing the ropes that swathed Silver. Silver merely said: "Taxi? Is it you? Well, how on earth—"

Then the man was free. As he rose, Taxi pushed the automatic of Plug Kennedy into his hands and thereby, as he suddenly felt, he transformed a helpless victim into a fighting power worth any three—yes, even if Barry Christian were one of them.

"Take this, Jim," he said. "You can use it better than I can."

"I don't know one end of an automatic from another," said the quiet voice of Silver. He did not even whisper! "Besides, they've not taken my guns. There's a strain of sentimentality in Barry Christian—and he left my guns here to go with me!"

He stepped to a table, and by the flicker of the firelight, Taxi saw the big man take possession of that pair of long-barreled Colts.

"Where are they? All towards the front of the house?" asked Silver.

"They are. We can get out the back way, Jim. You can whistle Parade to you. They've got him by this time, I suppose. But he'll break away when you whistle. And then we can run for it."

Silver put a hand on his arm.

"The house is going to blow up—*after* we're out of it. And then we'll have a pretty free hand to work on the crew of them, Taxi. Are you with me?"

Taxi stared through the dimness and the leap of the firelight at the big face. Even that dull light glinted on the silver spots of gray, like incipient horns, over the temples of Arizona Jim.

"I'm with you," said Taxi, "as long as I live—through everything!"

Silver kneeled by the remnant of the fuse and pinched it hard in three places under his heel, to make the powder burn more slowly. With a coal from the hearth, he lighted the end of it. Then he ran soundlessly with Taxi through the house, passing the open doors, one after another, until they had issued from the kitchen.

They kept on, for there was no need of much caution with the entire gang grouped about the front of the cabin. They reached the trees near the little shed which had been built as a stout lean-to against an outjutting of the rock.

And as they crouched in secure covert, the explosion struck at the ground under their feet, and the air beat with a soft, weighty hand at their faces.

The cabin split apart. A pale moon had just slid up above the eastern trees, and in that light and right across the face of the moon they could see free logs and beams from the house thrown high.

The blast was followed, after an instant, by the heavy thudding of the logs against the ground. The whole cabin lay flat, like a house of cards.

Still there was a little interval of silence, as though the watchers were stunned, then a wild outbreak of cheering voices. Guns were fired into the air in a steady thundering. Silver could see the gang capering under the moon with drunken happiness.

They were like silly youths on a spree. They interwove their arms and put back their heads and howled to the moon. They yelled themselves hoarse and, freshly tasting the cup of their happiness, yelled again. They danced in an Indian circle, prancing aimlessly up and down.

Only, apart from the rest, his arms folded, the moon gilding his long silken hair, Barry Christian faced the ruin and watched the thickening of the smoke that began to rise out of it.

Tongues of flame leaped. The blaze leaped and roared. It seemed a bonfire lighted to celebrate the grand occasion.

But it would take hours for that pile to burn down, and Taxi heard Barry Christian call his men together.

"We've made noise enough to call in any one within a mile from us. And now we've started a fire to show 'em the way. Boys, don't forget that we have a lot of gold dust packed away on that mule, in there. We've seen the last of Jim Silver, to-night, we've sent Taxi to another kind of hell, and now we can reward ourselves with a neat split of hard cash, for each of us, and scatter for the next job. Come on with me!"

They gathered together and followed him. Some of them kept turning back to stare at the fire and then stumbled forward again, blinded by the increasing brightness of the flames.

They passed into the open door of the shed, and Silver said, as a lantern was lighted in the interior of the shed:

"They've been collected there for us, Taxi. Lie low here in the brush. I'll get behind those rocks. We can make those fellows come out one by one with their hands over their heads, or else we can shoot that shack full of holes and get every man inside it that way. Keep the door covered, will you?"

Taxi slid into his place. The position was perfect. He was entirely covered. And the moon and the fire gave excellent light for shooting. He saw Silver get into place among a nest of rocks that would enable him to cover the door of the shed, also. There were no windows. That one point of exit was all that needed surveillance.

Then Silver's resonant voice rang out through the night: "Barry Christian! Oh, Barry Christian!"

There was a pause, and then a frightful cry from the shed: "Boys, the ghost of Silver has come for us."

CHAPTER XXV

A New Man

IF that had been the voice of Babe or any of his fellows, Taxi would not have been so stunned, but it was Barry Christian who had shouted out in a panic. It was incredible that that man should be weakened by superstition.

"Charlie Larue! Charlie Larue!" called Taxi. "I'm waiting out here for you."

"It's Taxi!" yelled Larue.

The lantern was dashed out in the shed. There was a confusion of voices inside, and then the louder tones of Pudge, explaining:

"I saw the detective walk off with him in handcuffs that he couldn't slip. I tell you, I *saw* it!"

Silver sang out: "You can't dodge us, boys. There's no way out of the shed except by that door. And if you try to stay inside, we'll turn the shack into a sieve and pepper the lot of you inside. Those of you who want to take your chances with the law can walk out of that door one by one, with your hands as high over your head as you can stretch them. Babe, you're first! Step out, and step fast, or we'll open up on you all."

There was another groaning confusion of voices. Then Babe appeared in the doorway with his hands above his head. He said:

"What a beating *I'm* going to soak up from Taxi!"

But he strode ahead to take his punishment, while Silver said:

"Walk right on into that patch of brush, and turn around before you get to it and back in. Taxi, get his guns and tie him."

Babe executed these orders with a perfect obedience, turned just before he reached the brush, and backed into it. When Taxi commanded him to put his hands behind his back, he obeyed, saying:

"You ain't going to get the same satisfaction, Taxi. You gotta use a club to get effects on me, and I used my hands on you. A club ain't got the same feeling."

Larue came next. He was completely gone. He stumbled halfway to the brush, and his knees seemed unwilling to support him.

"Poor Charlie!" said Babe. "You'd better've had it out with him back there in the Round-up Bar; better that than to hang for murdering Joe Feeley, which is what's going to happen to you, kid!"

Scotty came next, then Pokey, who refused to put his hands over his head and sauntered out with his hands in his pockets. His bravado lasted until he got into the brush. There he simply broke down and groaned and wept as Taxi tied him to the others.

Pudge came out, saying: "Play your luck where you find it!"

The Chinaman was next.

Silver said: "You yellow-skinned son of trouble, run out of here as fast as you can. I'm not going to bother about you."

The Chinaman bolted so fast that his pigtail stood straight out behind his head.

"Now, Christian!" called Silver. "Come out, old son!"

Barry Christian came, but he came in a style different from that of the others. He came with a six-gun in each hand, with his long hair flying, and dodged for cover, shooting at the same time toward the rocks and the brush.

Taxi, taking a good aim, pulled his trigger. There was only a dull clicking sound for answer. He knew that his gun had jammed, and in another moment Barry Christian was out of sight.

"Jim! Jim!" cried Taxi. "What's the matter? My gun jammed—but what's the matter with you?"

Silver walked over to him, shaking his head.

"Listen!" he said.

Far away, they could hear the departing thudding of hoofs as Barry Christian mounted a mustang and fled through the night.

"I couldn't do it," said Silver. "It wasn't a fair fight.

And when he charged out like that, ready to die—well, letting him go is the worst deal I ever gave the world in all my days, but I couldn't help it."

Of course, the report of that escape was twisted. Nothing did so much to lower the reputation of Silver; nothing did so much to raise the fame of Barry Christian, afterwards, as the fact that the outlaw had fought his way through great odds and escaped with his life. That his followers were lost mattered very little.

It was well after daylight before the procession got into Horseshoe Flat. The whole town was roused. The elements of peace and order had kept their heads low for a long time, while the gang of Barry Christian was near enough to dominate the place. They turned out in force now, and lodged the outlaws in their little newly-built jail.

Justice and a stern law waited for every one of those men except Charlie Larue. His nerve, which had first been broken by Taxi in the Round-up Bar, failed him completely when the iron door of his cell was locked. That night he used his belt to hang himself to the bars of his cell rather than await a judge, a jury, and a State hangman.

There was one curious little aftermath the next day when Mr. Kennedy, the detective, returned to his hunting grounds. The townsmen, of course, knew why he had come, and before he walked three blocks from the station, a crowd had commenced to gather. They trailed Kennedy to the door of the Creighton lodging house and then they swarmed over him.

When his hands were tied, he had the privilege of seeing Taxi wave to him from a front window of the house, with Silver and the girl standing beside him. Then Kennedy was taken back to catch the next train out.

Certain things were said in Kennedy's ear by leading townsmen of Horseshoe Flat. They were vigorous enough to assure that he would never take his chances in that town again. Whatever Taxi had been before, said Horseshoe Flat, he was a new man now. And the West is the place where the past is forgotten, and the world is given new men for old.

Taxi, back in the Creighton boarding house, finished

the just division of the gold dust which Barry Christian had looted from the Feeley mine. The majority of Horseshoe Flat was up there in the hills prospecting for a new strike and finding a few streaks of color and little more to boast of. But Taxi and Silver were splitting the treasure into three parts. Half, they decided, went to the mother and the rest of the family of Joe Feeley. The other half was divided between Silver and Taxi. Sally Creighton weighed out the gold on a kitchen scales, very equitably.

Then Silver said: "You've turned a corner, Taxi. You're on a new street. You may think that you're hitched to your past, but you're not. Horseshoe Flat wants you, and Horseshoe Flat will kick the rest of the world in the face if it tries to get at you. You have the money for a new start. There's Sally here, who knows how to keep house and cook. She can tell you how to live on the new street, if you want to settle down in this part of the world."

Taxi looked her straight in the eye. "Sally," he said, "do you hear that? Do you think that you could fit a yegg and a crook into your life?"

"Not for a minute," she said. "But I could fit Taxi into my life forever."

They kept looking at one another, smiling like children. Then Silver said:

"I'd better leave, because you'll have to do something about that, Taxi."

Taxi reached out a hand and caught his arm.

"When you go, I'm going with you," he said. "You people trust me, but I don't trust myself. If you hammer me long enough, maybe I'll break. Jim, let me ride with you for three months. If you still think I'm right at the end of that time, I'm coming back."

"What do you say to that, Sally?" asked Jim Silver.

"Why," she said, "isn't it fair and square? He can't realize the new idea all at once. Jim, can we expect him to know himself as well as we know him?"